"Brad Listi uses sharp, crystalline prose to navigate through moments of failure, love, fatherhood, psychedelics, and the unknown. What does it mean to be an artist, a husband, a father? This novel's reach toward meaning and understanding is truly unforgettable—I loved this book."—**CHELSEA HODSON**, author of *Tonight I'm Someone Else*

"I highly enjoyed *Be Brief and Tell Them Everything*, which I found funny and entertaining but also moving, serious, tender, and contemplative. It lives up to its title."—**TAO LIN**, author of *Leave Society*

"It's a wonder the long-awaited second novel by Brad Listi didn't kill him—or at least render him mad. Instead, he's produced an enduring work of art and a moving guide to truth, love, and perseverance."
—**MARCY DERMANSKY**, author of *Very Nice*

"We already knew that Brad Listi was a master of listening. His podcasts are a model for anyone: Brad asks a question and then is silent, and his silence draws us in. What we didn't know is that Brad also listens while writing, that he can draw life in all its nakedness, in all its mystery, with all its pain and hope, into the pages of a book. That even when he speaks about himself, he holds the microphone out to the world."—**ANDREA BAJANI**, author of *If You Kept a Record of Sins*

Be Brief
and
Tell Them
Everything

Be Brief
and
Tell Them
Everything

Brad Listi

PUBLISHING

New York, NY

Ig Publishing
Box 2547
New York, NY 10163
www.igpub.com

ISBN: 978-1-63246-13-6-0

PRINTED IN THE UNITED STATES OF AMERICA

FIRST EDITION | FIRST PRINTING

To Kari, Evan, and River

If you write for God you will reach many men and bring them joy. If you write for men— you may make some money and you may give someone a little joy and you may make a noise in the world, for a little while. If you write for yourself, you can read what you yourself have written and after ten minutes you will be so disgusted that you will wish that you were dead

—Thomas Merton

Short poem: be brief and tell us everything.

—Charles Simic

THIS BOOK TOOK twelve years to write. It started out as a novel and then it became a different novel and then it was another, different novel and then it was an essay collection and then it was nothing for a while and then it was a memoir and then it became a novel again and now it's whatever this is.

During the time it took to write this book, I met my wife, Franny, dated her, proposed to her, married her. We got a French bulldog and named him Walter. The global economy collapsed. Franny got pregnant and gave birth to a girl we named Alice. A close friend died of an accidental opiate overdose. I wrote a screenplay called *Man of Letters*, an absurd comedy about a forty-year-old spoken word poet who lives with his parents. It didn't sell. I produced five hundred episodes of a podcast called *Otherppl with Brad Listi* in which I talk at length with other writers. We suffered through five miscarriages. I co-wrote a sitcom that sold but was never made. I worked several different media jobs and referred to myself in public as a "creative consultant." We finally conceived a second child, a little boy named Oscar—joy!—and then, six months after his birth, he was diagnosed with cerebral palsy and epilepsy. Heartbreak.

Also: Walter choked on a bagel and died. This was years ago. Franny gave him the Heimlich and we rushed him to the vet, but he didn't make it.

We now have another dog, a rescue mutt from Mexico. Alice named her Twiggy. She was born in a litter of eleven puppies and abandoned in the streets of Tijuana.

·

We live in Los Angeles, a city about which almost everyone has something stupid to say. Seventy-two suburbs in search of a city. Makes the rest of California seem authentic. The plastic asshole of the world, William Faulkner called it.

I've been here almost twenty years. Franny has been here since college.

It's like living on a soundstage, I sometimes say. And people who have never been here before like to tell you they can't stand it here.

•

The truth is that I've never felt like I fully belong here. But then who can be said to fully belong here. The region on its own terms should be, by rights, a mostly arid expanse of coastal sage and chaparral— but instead there exists an improbable, teeming metropolis, covering nearly 500 square miles. It is a city almost entirely without visual logic, no apparent unifying theme, no plan or system of organization. Walk out your front door and turn right or turn left, and within minutes you will encounter all manner of architectural possibilities, a chaotic hodgepodge, a warehouse, a church, a strip club, a Frank Gehry building. It makes no sense. And I suppose this is the point. The unifying theme of Los Angeles is that there is no unifying theme, the point is that there is no point. Everything is here and all of it is jumbled together and none of it is related to anything. Be whoever you want to be. Live however you want to live. Scrap and claw and fight and dream, and pretend to be infinite in your infinity pool. On some level, I'm able to appreciate it. On another level, I'm appalled.

•

Occasionally I'll tell myself that I should move my family out to the country, far off the beaten path, live someplace sleepy and beautiful, Oregon or Montana or Idaho or Colorado, tucked away up in the mountains, a small-town aerie under big sky. That or I should try to find work overseas in a place like Sweden or Denmark or Norway or New Zealand, where the happiness indices are reportedly high and infrastructure and education are supposedly first-rate, where government, rumor has it, functions with a reasonable degree of efficacy and where life would be, for us, I imagine, both simpler and more exotic at the same time.

Maybe we should get out of here, I'll say to Franny. Go be sane somewhere. But to do it, we'll have to be bold. Anything normal feels crazy anymore. Try to give the kids an experience. Some kind of alpine village with a bookstore and a decent café. That's all I want. I'm not greedy.

The two of us lying in bed, flat on our backs, staring up into the blankness of the ceiling.

Maybe Switzerland, I'll say, dreaming. It's expensive, on the one hand. But insulated and picturesque and trilingual.

Let's be neutral, Franny will say. Neutral and extremely calm.

The thing that haunts me, I'll say, is this feeling that we're living through a uniquely stupid period in history. To be in opposition seems rational. But to actually do it, you have to take action. You can't just sit around *talking* all the time. Otherwise what? The whole thing's so embarrassing. And that's really the word for it all. You wake up in the morning and you pick up your phone to read the news, and you feel ashamed to be alive.

.

The conversation might then return to Switzerland, with talk of orderliness and air quality and the children able to play outside unsupervised. Cattle bells sounding in the valley. Universal healthcare. Bullet trains to France. But soon enough the fantasy will become unwieldy, collapsing under its own cartoonish weight, and I'll find myself conceding that the logistics are overwhelming, not to mention the price tag, and anyway geography rarely changes anything anyhow.

And this is where I always wind up, I'll say. The real trouble is between my ears, and I know it. Imagine being miserable in the Alps, drinking hot cocoa, feeling like something's *missing*. Which is exactly what would happen. But on some level I refuse to believe it. . . .

And so on.

.

And beyond that, of course, there would also be the issue of Oscar and his therapies and how living in any kind of remote location would likely be a nonstarter anyhow, as access to facilities and expert medical care is, for us, essential. And what about the language barrier? Taking such matters into consideration, our life in Los Angeles can be seen as a remarkable stroke of luck.

Imagine, we'll sometimes say to each other, what happens to disabled kids who don't have access to resources. Parents left to their own devices. Families in dire circumstances, in jungles and mud huts and dismal urban slums. What about *them*? Who's looking out for *those* poor kids? And meanwhile here we are, alive in a kind of paradise, dreaming about escape, nursing our wounds in a city where the weather—at least for now, anyway—barely ever changes. Yes, it's completely insane here. But for the most part it beats the alternative.

.

Los Angeles is a complete mess, I'll say to Franny. It's a terrible place to raise children. But a piece of wood doesn't become smooth by rubbing it with velvet.

Over the years this has become one of my go-to lines, something I read in a Buddhism book once, a nice little way to rationalize our decision to raise our kids in the eye of the storm. Though the question it begs is always one of proportion: *Just how much sandpaper are we talking about here?*

•

Back when Franny was pregnant with Alice, I remember telling her, as we stood in the kitchen one night, how happy I was that we were having a baby. A sweet moment in a young marriage. The two of us, hugging by the stove. The roundness of her belly pressing against mine.

I don't always realize that it's happening, I said, but every once in a while it hits me, and I just want you to know that I'm excited about it.

You are?

I am.

How so?

I don't know. I just am. It'll be fun to hang out with her.

What are you going to do with her?

I'm going to . . . share all of my wisdom with her.

Franny thought about it for a moment.

And what are you going to do the next day? she said.

•

The truth is that I don't know what, exactly, to do. Ultimately there are no clean answers. We have to make our decisions and deal with the consequences. We live here, and most likely we'll continue to live here, barring some unforeseen development. What matters most, we tell ourselves, is what happens at home: the manners we enforce, the values we champion, who we teach our kids to be by virtue of our own examples.

And surely this is true enough. Still, I can't help but wonder what this city might be doing to us, how it might be taking its toll. Has it robbed us of some critical perspective? Is sincerity even possible here? Can the mood of the place be avoided, the common Hollywood affect, the weary knowingness about everything, the cynical eye-roll at all of the cultural stupidities and excesses, even as one might participate in them and profit from them? Is it possible to live a life apart from this, within city limits, or are we all simply doomed to embody it, marching through our sun-bleached days, alive inside the machine? Or am I being melodramatic, tying myself into knots? This desire to be sure about things: a kind of fear. Maybe the wiser strategy would be to relinquish all prophecies of doom. Stop having so many opinions, and relax a bit. Lose the certainty. It's nothing more than hubris anyhow. As if I actually know what this is, or where the world is headed. Please.

.

I am, as best I understand it, the cosmos grown to self-awareness, an assemblage of infinite parts. Every thought I've ever had, every bite of food I've ever eaten, the sunlight, the birds, the rain, the trees—all of it locked together in an endless causal chain.

And here I am.

Nonlocal.

I live in a place where the light pollution is so bad, you can barely see the stars.

Bewilderment.

Always best to respond to the quandary with something approaching lucid indifference. Bear witness, stay calm, and describe. Write it down. My distant ancestors were microbes, fish, mice, and arboreal apes, and every atom in my body is traceable to the explosion of high-mass stars, billions of years ago. Fair enough. The best I can hope for is to live for a century inside the mystery, hopefully in a state of relative comfort, take care of my wife and kids, and then die as everyone before me has died, absorbed, most likely, into an oblivion so total that I can't even begin to fully comprehend it.

Or maybe that's wrong.

Beats the shit out of me.

A WHILE BACK, I interviewed Tim O'Brien for my podcast. National Book Award winner and author of the classic story collection *The Things They Carried.* O'Brien was seventy-five at the time. I found him to be wise, unpretentious, hugely likable. He showed up at my door on a Wednesday morning dressed in a baseball cap, a sweater, blue jeans, a bomber jacket, a pack of Carltons in his pocket. He burned through two of them before the interview, flicking his ashes in the driveway. We then went into the garage and sat across from each other for more than an hour, talking easily about all manner of things, including his military service in Vietnam, which forms the basis for much of his work.

At one point, he was telling me about landmines, setting out on foot into the jungle, a young man in his twenties, sweating bullets, afraid that every step could spell his doom. As he was talking, I found myself thinking, of all things, about this book, my many failed attempts to write this book, and how over the years, in trying to write this book, *another goddamned version of this book*, I developed a certain edginess— creative anxiety mixed with creeping dread. This, I'm embarrassed to admit, was where my head went. A decorated combat vet and canonical author, describing in careful detail his near-death experiences in the fog of war. And me, thinking about my midlife creative troubles, my stupid little champagne problems.

At the time, the book was really bothering me. And O'Brien, with his way of speaking in complete paragraphs, accidentally illuminated my difficulties. This basic idea of moving through a landscape slowly, with a gathering sense of dread, afraid to step—it resonated. The long and ridiculous struggle I had endured, trying to write something coherent. And how the process, over the years, had repeatedly been disrupted by calamity. How I would settle on an approach and be writing on a regular schedule, determined to see it through, and then, *boom,* something else would happen: another miscarriage, another untimely death, another diagnosis, some godawful job stress, what have you. Something in my life would explode, and the shockwaves would send me spinning into a different orbit. Whatever version I had been working on would suddenly seem alien, absurd, unrecognizable. That or I would tell myself that I had arrived at some other, better idea—a brand new shiny object—and off I would go in pursuit.

•

Years ago, there was a version called *Happiness is Chemical*. A novel, roughly 80,000 words, a disjointed screwball comedy about a guy named Bill Tippet, a self-loathing high school chemistry teacher whose dog is dying of cancer.

As the story unfolds, Bill has a fling with a colleague, the new art teacher, a blue-eyed redhead named Rose Carmody, a functional alcoholic with a sketchy ex-boyfriend. One night after school they get extremely drunk together and have bad sex at Rose's house and pass out. Bill, who normally isn't a big drinker, wets the bed in his sleep, and when he wakes up in the middle of the night and realizes what he's done, he panics and tries to cover it up by dumping a bucket of water on her. He pretends to be in party mode. The whole thing spirals badly.

Rose wakes up from a blackout to find Bill standing over her with a bucket in his hands. She's soaking wet, disoriented, frightened. In her inebriated state, she conflates Bill with her sketchy ex-boyfriend, pulls some pepper spray from her nightstand drawer, and fires it into his eyes. Bill drops to the floor, writhing, and eventually flees in the nude. The following day, in a terrible state of humiliation, he writes Rose a rambling letter of apology, attempting to explain himself. The sketchy ex-boyfriend gets ahold of it. Chaos ensues.

I finished the book, roughly 300 pages, in a frantic, ten-week push and emailed it to my agent.

It's about a chemistry teacher, I told her, *who has very little chemistry with anyone.*

To my surprise, my agent read quickly, responding by the end of the week.

I love the LA elements, she said, *and I love the disaster at Christmas, and the emergency room set piece, but I'm desperate for something to go right for this guy. (The dog dying is almost too much.) I just don't know if I have any faith that life is going to get better for him, and I really need it to.*

In response to this appraisal, I quickly shifted gears and started hacking away at the manuscript, thinking I could mold it into something else entirely, something better, more commercial, less depressing—and hopefully in quick turnaround. I was calling it *The Dog Has a Problem.* Gone were Rose Carmody and the bucket and the pepper spray, all of it excised in favor of a heavily streamlined narrative about a solitary man and his dog—and eventually there would be a woman. The basic structure was set. A romantic comedy of sorts—a story lighter and more playful than its predecessor. At the beginning of the book, it was just the man and his dog, so it was a very lonely period for the man. The problem, I found, was that the dog couldn't talk, so there was no dialogue. It was just the man, all by himself, overthinking everything in the presence of his dog. I worked on this version for about six weeks before abandoning it in a state of terrible frustration.

It's obnoxious, I wrote in one of my notebooks during the aftermath, *not to mention brutally funny, to focus all of this energy and attention on a single pursuit, to the exclusion and neglect of pretty much everything else in life, only to have the pursuit end, again, in utter failure, amounting to absolutely nothing at all, just another meaningless creative implosion, another stupid turd down the drain.*

•

The most spectacular of the failed iterations was something called, for lack of a better title, *The Kidney Book*. It was a novel about a desperate man caught inside the grim logic of hyper-capitalism. Here again the hero was named Bill Tippet, but this time he was a down-on-his-luck novelist from New Orleans. In a desperate attempt to free himself from credit card debt, he tries to sell one of his kidneys to a dying stranger in Israel for $300,000 in cash. In the end he winds up giving away his kidney for free.

The plot was inspired by a magazine article I'd read, a profile of a real estate mogul and "moral extremist" from Philadelphia named Zell Kravinsky, a man who had given away his entire fortune, more than $45 million, and then, in a finishing move, gave away one of his kidneys. His family and friends tried to stop him but he could not be dissuaded. He marched into Albert Einstein Medical Center and offered up a kidney for free. Doctors on staff sent him to a psychiatrist to confirm that he was of sound mind. Yes, Kravinsky assured them. He was serene.

I'm not generous and I'm not insane, he later told reporters. Maybe the sanest thing I do is give things away.

·

I worked on this version for more than a year, completing an entire draft, and even went to Israel for research. I had never been to Israel before and felt I needed to see the place in order to write about it with authority. As a gentile with limited understanding, it seemed like the logical move. This was how I couched it to myself, and how I sold it to Franny, convinced that my novel needed an exotic locale to give it added heft. *Man Goes to Holy Land to Sell Kidney*. Plus, I had read somewhere on the internet that the underground market for kidneys was particularly strong in Israel. And so it was settled. I packed a bag and flew halfway around the world for a four-day weekend, spending thousands of dollars in the process, and Franny, God bless her, gave me her blessing. Alice was just a baby at the time, having recently celebrated her first birthday. Oscar was still a dream. We had recently suffered through our first miscarriage, at week six.

In Tel Aviv, I stayed at a Sheraton on the waterfront, my room looking out to the sea. The city, I decided, felt like Miami, a Middle Eastern version of Miami, *Miami but with consequences*, and my experiences of it, heavily colored by jet lag, involved aimlessly riding a bike all over town, stuffing my face with hummus and pita, and sitting listlessly on park benches in the shade of large sycamore trees. I took dozens of photos, mostly out of a sense of obligation, and spoke haltingly, with embarrassment, into my iPhone's voice recorder, as if I were an actor who had been hired to play the role of Writer but had suddenly forgotten my lines.

Using Google Maps, I found my way to Sourasky Medical Center, a sprawling hospital on Weizmann Street, hoping to tour it, thinking it might be the setting for my novel's black market kidney transplant, but the entrance was heavily guarded. Two young men with machine guns scowled and turned me away.

I left.

After pedaling for a while, I stopped off at a small café where, in a state of increasing despondence, I ordered a quadruple espresso, connected to the Wi-Fi, and watched a YouTube video about a Moldovan man, an emaciated shepherd with an eighth-grade education, whose kidney had been removed for $7,000—three thousand less than he was promised, and twenty-five hundred of it turned out to be counterfeit. The money was now long gone, he said, and he lived in a van next to a pigsty. His remaining kidney gave him trouble on a regular basis and often caused him excruciating pain.

The only way out is death, he said.

•

On the third day, I caught a cab to Jerusalem, a $150 ride, almost three thousand feet of elevation gain, the weather much cooler on the plateau. After checking in at my hotel, I immediately set out for the Old City, entering through the Jaffa Gate on foot. Winding my way through the narrow, labyrinthine alleyways—food stands, clothing stores, tchotchke shops, *a mall with a biblical aesthetic*—I eventually found my way to the Western Wall, where it immediately became clear that I didn't know how to feel. It was a wall. I had seen this wall before, dozens if not hundreds of times, across various media, but now, faced with the actual reality of

The Wall, I wasn't quite sure what to do. I went to take a selfie but was reprimanded with comical immediacy by a stern-faced Jewish elder in orthodox garb who seemed to materialize, ghostlike, at my side, bearded, offended, hissing at me in Hebrew, motioning for me to put my phone away.

I apologized in English, confused, then turned and retreated, head-down, across the plaza, ducking into an alleyway, looking at my phone, surprised to find the ill-conceived selfie—I didn't realize I'd actually taken one—my sweaty face lodged into the lower-left corner of the frame, badly out of focus, with The Wall in the background, sharp and clear against the blue sky. I texted it to Franny as I moved, sending her the blurry image, along with the accompanying message I AM HERE, in all caps.

•

That night, already the final night of my trip, I ate dinner alone at a sidewalk café near the Mamilla Mall, drinking red wine, devouring a basket of bread, watching the pedestrians, listening to rap music blaring from the passing cars—all of it happening, I told myself, just a stone's throw from Golgotha, where the crucifixion, it was said, had taken place more than two thousand years ago.

In my notebook I wrote:

There is a high-end shopping mall leading into the Old City at the Jaffa Gate. And inside of the city walls, not far from the Via Dolorosa, there are dead animals hanging by their hooves and gift shops selling Jesus Christ bobblehead dolls. I am currently listening to "Regulate" by Warren G and Nate Dogg. It is the twenty-first century AD. I just ate an entire loaf of bread.

Moments later, after a brief exchange with my waiter, I admitted to myself that my novel was probably dead. A gut-level feeling, dreadful and strong. The book wasn't working and it wasn't going to work and I could see it all very clearly now. It would never work because it would never be funny. It needed to be at least a little bit funny in order to work. But I knew I couldn't find a way to make it funny. Maybe somebody else could do it, but I couldn't. And I didn't want to.

Desperate people, dying or impoverished, trying to buy and sell organs. The whole thing was just depressing. It depressed me. I felt asinine. Empty of intent. I set my fork down, looking blankly out at the street, the pedestrians going by, the flow of auto traffic. A truck pulled up in front of the restaurant, engine coughing. The rattling tailpipe. Gasoline odor. Exhaust. I brought a hand to my mouth and stared down at my plate, at the pile of noodles, untouched.

·

On the flight home, I wrote the following in my notebook:

In the end, all art is about the artist's personal struggle, and whenever I get away from this essential fact, I lose interest. I lose the thread. Feel phony. Go adrift. The most critical thing is to tell the truth, even if it's fiction (especially if it's fiction), even though it's impossible to ever do such a thing. You can never tell the full truth, but you try. And this is the project. It's about the attempt. Maybe kids can do it. Adults can't. This is why kids' art is charming. Maybe the only way to do it as an adult is to write something that will never be read. Write your story as honestly as you can, include every lingering guilt and scalding shame, share it with no one, and—

The entry ends here, in abrupt fashion, followed only by the word "turbulence," written in a wobbly hand a couple of lines below. We were somewhere over the Atlantic at that point, rocketing westward at cruising altitude, when the plane hit an air pocket and was jolted so dramatically that multiple passengers screamed and a flight attendant sustained a minor head injury. The captain came on over the intercom to apologize, assuring us that the episode was temporary and they were searching for a smoother ride. The choppiness continued for another ten minutes or so before finally, mercifully abating.

Rattled by the experience, I ordered a double-bourbon and proceeded to watch several movies back-to-back, including a documentary about Bob Marley, the conclusion of which detailed the reggae legend's tragic demise in 1981, of skin cancer. There was the ominous marking under one of his toenails. A dark vertical stripe. A doctor recommended immediate amputation. Marley, citing his religious beliefs, refused.

He died. Age thirty-six. His legacy secure.

His last words: *Money can't buy life.*

•

Hours later, when the plane touched down in Los Angeles, it was midmorning, bright and hot, a milieu not dissimilar to the one I'd left in Israel. I caught a cab back home and found Franny in the bedroom, working with her laptop resting on her belly. Almost exactly as I had left her four days ago. Alice was in the nursery, napping. I dropped my bag. A weary kiss. We talked about my trip for a few minutes. I lied and told her it had gone very well, that I had gotten what I needed and was excited about my progress. I then went into the bathroom to shower, and after my shower, while standing at the sink, I glanced down at my thumbnail and saw a brown stripe and thought: *No.*

Was the stripe really brown? And did it even qualify as a stripe? Maybe it was purplish.

In a state of controlled panic, I dressed and went to my computer and conducted the dreaded Google search. Subungual melanoma. Rare. Fast-growing. Almost always lethal. The images were, to my eye, irrefutable. I held my thumb up, matching it against the unlucky thumbs, and my breathing turned shallow.

This was it. This was my story. The shape of my narrative, coming clear. The turbulence had been an omen. My time in the Holy Land suddenly filled with poetic meaning.

·

The next forty-eight hours were a kind of charade. A try-ing-to-seem-normal, a pretending-to-be-busy. Focusing on work as much as I could. More plaintive than usual in my alone moments. A doomed man's attention to detail. The birdsong, the wind, the whistling mailman, the trees. I rocked Alice for an extra-long time before setting her into her crib at night. I mentioned nothing about my condition to Franny, figuring I wouldn't give her the news until I'd gotten the doctor's official word.

·

On the morning of my appointment, I arrived early and filled out the necessary paperwork. No small talk. Coiled, quiet, terrified, polite. I was escorted into an examination room by a sleepy-eyed receptionist with long acrylic nails. There I stood, stripped down to my underwear, waiting to receive the news of my fate. Minutes later, when the doctor entered the room and asked me how I was doing, it was as though I'd been uncorked. Instantly I lost my cool and started rambling about Israel, the documentary, Bob Marley, all of it. She squinted a little, looked down at my thumb, and laughed in my face. She told me it was only a bruise.

You're sure? I said. Completely?

That's correct, she said, pressing my nail with the pad of her thumb. You're not dying. It's okay. You'll survive.

She then gave me a once-over, scanning my body for any problematic moles, and everything checked out just fine. That was it. Appointment over. Clean bill of health. The doctor wished me well, instructed me to relax, and made her exit. I remained in place for a while, alone in my briefs, staring out the window to the hills in the distance. Once again entirely wrong about something. And happy, for a change, to be mistaken. The shape of my narrative, unknown. The cause of my end, a living mystery.

.

A few minutes later, driving back across town, I couldn't help but notice the giddiness within me, the flood of relief, the narcotic bliss of averted death. The sky extra blue, the flowers bursting, everything humming with magic. Heading east on Santa Monica Boulevard, I played some Bob Marley on the stereo. And why not? "Time Will Tell." High volume. *Money can't buy life.* The words took on a new resonance. It was clear to me now what must have been painfully clear to Bob in 1981: that life on the precipice of death is poverty in its harshest and most essential form. Here I was, nearly forty years old—older than Marley when his light had gone out—a husband and a father and a man of many jobs, a writer in the throes of enormous frustration. I had just flown to Israel on a four-day boondoggle and returned home empty-handed. And what of it? The money was spent. It was of limited utility anyhow. There was no sense staying mired in self-recrimination, no sense fixating on anything for too long, no sense worrying about all the things that I'd done or hadn't done or never would do. The only thing that mattered in the end was the fact that it was only a bruise.

I DON'T WANT to waste my life, I once tweeted. I meant it as a joke, self-deprecatory, ironic. This was before I quit Twitter, to which I was addicted and which, along with the rest of the internet, had essentially destroyed my capacity for sustained attention.

I was at the gym, of all places, when it ended. Early morning, predawn, midwinter. I had just done some sit-ups in a little anteroom off the main gym, where people sometimes shadowboxed and pounded on the heavy bags. Lying on my back, staring up into my phone, scrolling through the miserable feed. Half-asleep and middle-aged and working on my core. In a moment of impulse, I deleted my account. A kind of modern suicide. No official announcement or attempt at explanation—not that anyone cared. Instead I just quietly died.

.

A few days later, on the podcast, I spoke of it a bit in the monologue, assuring my listeners that I wasn't lost in a mental health crisis—an indicator, if there ever was one, of just how upside-down things had gotten when it came to this stuff. The decision to quit social media, so often perceived as a raving cry for help rather than a declaration of sanity. Certain people might tell you that you were a fool for leaving, that you were doing grave damage to your "brand." That or they'd mock you, predicting that you'd soon come crawling back for another fix. Most likely of all, they would imply, either directly or indirectly, that you were a smug and self-satisfied scold.

And fair enough. I'll admit to a little smugness in those first few days. It's hard not to succumb to some triumphalism when you've finally managed to disentangle yourself from this stuff. I remember telling friends how relieved I was, how much better I felt, how my brain was coming back to me. If I sounded like a man in recovery, glowing with the conviction of a recent convert, it's because I was. Yes, there are those of us who can use social media in moderation, picking their spots. I was never one of them. I was an addict, full-blown. These sites—Twitter, for me, in particular—had consumed an entire decade of my life. More than anything, I felt embarrassed about it. Embarrassed that I ever allowed a pack of sociopathic dweebs from Silicon Valley to manipulate my reality, to fuck with my dopamine levels, to monetize my personal information, replicating the details of my identity and selling them back to me as products and services. Embarrassed that the soulless "growth hackers" had me agitated for so long, using their jiggered algorithms to "keep me on the platform" and undo my capacity to think. *Fuck this stupid bullshit*, I said to myself as I lay there on the floor of the gym that morning. *Fuck all of it. Fuck everyone. I quit.*

And I did.

And didn't go back. It wasn't entirely easy, either. Addictive tech is addictive on purpose, and far more mainstream, by an order of magnitude, than any street drug in history. Almost everyone I knew was dependent on it to some degree, whether they realized it or not. One of the greatest and most sinister feats of modern capitalism. And amazing to think of how quickly it happened. Ten, fifteen years—that was all it took. By then they had most everybody, myself included. All of us walking around, dive-bombing into our phones, lost inside our information silos, eyes glued to our screens, unable to tolerate even the smallest moments of inertia. The digitized equivalent of a nicotine hit.

It was impossible to know how much money they had made off of me, or how thoroughly they had strip-mined my existence. The truth was that I was less concerned about handing over the scattered contents of my brain than I was with the brain-scattering itself. For ten solid years, I had willingly participated in what amounted to a massive, unregulated psychological experiment, the safety of which was far from clear. I couldn't help but believe that it had done some damage. The behaviors that it asked you to engage in were, in the aggregate, such a toxic and exhausting slog. The nonstop news feed. The distorted view of reality that it presented. The ongoing project of monitoring how people felt about you, and how you felt about people. How obnoxious that was. How relentless and tedious and juvenile. And how any random, waking moment of your life, when shared, was reduced to a data point in cyberspace. How many likes? How many retweets? How many comments? What's the feedback? The constant checking in, the neurotic obsessing, hoping that the world would approve.

•

I'm done trying to create impressions of myself, I told Franny. I've retired. It's what these sites make you do. It becomes your job. There isn't any choice. Which is the whole point. Always packaging yourself for an audience.

Franny said nothing, only nodded a little. My agita

often seemed to confuse her. She had never really gotten into social media in any kind of serious way. Instagram only, and never on a regular basis. A private account. Innocuous pics of the kids, here and there.

Anyway, I said. I'm all done. It's over. Finally. No more bullshit. No more narcissistic reward.

I paused for a moment, thinking on it, before conceding that my decision to quit would likely hurt my podcast, and might affect my writing life, my ability to find work as a consultant. What was the new rule of thumb? *If you're not online, you don't exist.* Almost certainly it would cost me something—how much, exactly, was anyone's guess—but the upside, I felt, would be worth it.

.

Embedded within this admission was a kind of surrender, a confession of how tired I felt. Tired of logging on. Tired of hustling. Tired of everybody hustling. Tired of being asked to click this link, or buy this book, or donate to somebody's GoFundMe so their cousin could go on dialysis. The constant emotional tumult. The endless process of trying to win approval, do good, be right, react. The exhausting salesmanship in every direction. Everybody curating their semifictional selves, selves that were always designed, however subtly, to be superior to the actual thing. The eternal game of one-upmanship. Everybody on a major quest to become a minor god. *And we wonder why people are anxious all the time.*

.

Then there was the simple issue of attention span. Brain health. How fragmented I often felt. How hard it had become to stay focused on anything. To read actual books. Yes, I got stuff done. Yes, I was able to function. But the impacts that social media had were not small. All too often, my work life amounted to a constant toggling between the task at hand and my Twitter feed. I knew that I was scattered, acting like a lab rat, but rationalized the behavior as a form of productivity, telling myself that by "maintaining a presence" I was contributing to the larger project. Never mind that it was unpaid labor, often adding up to hours of my day. What propelled me was the notion that it was somehow leading up to something, and could be leveraged at a later date and made good—but only, of course, if I somehow found a way to crack the code, go viral, escape the meager realm of the average user and amass an absurd number of followers. To get there, I'd have to work at it, and be satisfied with compensation of an entirely virtual nature: those little hits of dopamine, those tiny masturbations of self-esteem. And meanwhile the overlords at Twitter would be laughing and lining their pockets with actual cash, cruising up to Napa in their Teslas, flying over to Thailand for a ten-day silent retreat.

.

If there was a central flaw in my logic, it was probably the fact that I was never really "good" at social media to begin with. None of it ever came easily to me. I didn't really know how to do it. No knack. I would tweet things like "Abraham LinkedIn" and feel the collective eye-roll. It likely had something to do with my age. Generation X. The last generation to experience a (mostly) analog childhood. Yes, I had adapted to digital life, but only as an adult, which seemed meaningful. The shift began in college and accelerated thereafter. Social media had arrived when I was thirty—a disruption to my reality, rather than reality itself. Young enough to participate, but old enough to remember a time of rotary dial telephones. And now here I was, up to my neck in it, at large in a world of selfies and influencers and bottomless psychological need. Like a dad in pleated khakis, crashing a crowded house party.

.

In many ways it felt like an echo of something I'd been telling myself throughout my adult life: that

I was fundamentally maladaptive, an oddball, that while I looked like a relatively ordinary guy, I was, in fact, a kind of freak. I didn't fit. And never had. But was this *actually* true? Or was it just convenient bullshit, a common sentiment made into a crutch, a tidy little blanket excuse for any shortcoming? There were, I reasoned, people like this in the world. There *were* oddballs. And maybe I was one of them. Whatever traditional structures existed, maybe they weren't meant to accommodate me. And vice versa. Nothing theatrical about it. No self-pity. Possibly just a statement of fact. Maybe, in the scheme of things, I was an ogre. Reasonably good-natured. Somewhat monkish in temperament. Able to fake it okay. And concerned, especially lately, about pissing my life away on stupid bullshit.

An ordinary middle-aged reckoning. Right on time.

The first half of my existence had been spent, with only moderate success, trying to become someone, and the back half would be spent learning to become no one. And this was fine with me. In fact, this sounded *good* to me. It sounded sane. It sounded like ambition in its proper form. *Learn how to disintegrate. Learn how to let it all go.* What other project was there, in the end? If nothing else, it felt like a necessary repudiation of all the market-driven manias, the insanities of modern hustle culture. Everybody trying to "own the moment," whatever the fuck that meant.

Everybody becoming a propagandist for their own fate. All of it rooted, it seemed to me, in the bedrock of sadness and fear. The desperate human quest to fill the void.

.

This was the general tenor of my thinking on that morning in the gym when I quit Twitter. A kind of culminating moment, though on the surface there was nothing too dramatic about it. A grown man laid out on his back, on an exercise mat, staring up into the depths of his phone and pressing DELETE. Done. I continued with my workout, finished it, went home. Showered, ate breakfast, kissed the kids. I walked out to my office in the garage, opened up my laptop and set about my day.

At the time, I was doing some contract work for one of my clients, helping to deliver an audio documentary series on iconic American food products. Deadline rapidly approaching. I had been assigned an episode devoted to the Twinkie. My day would be spent cutting together interviews with current and former Hostess executives and the descendants of the late James Dewar, who invented the beloved snack cake at the height of the Great Depression. There was, as well, the issue of sourcing appropriate music and digging through a file of archival materials provided by the production company that hired me. Among this material was a Twinkie commercial from the 1980s, featuring schoolchildren speculating on how the snack cake achieved its creamy filling. The first time I watched it, I was stunned to realize that I knew almost every single word, verbatim. Nearly forty years had passed since I'd last laid eyes on this thing or given it even the slightest bit of thought, and yet there it all was, fully intact, called up from the depths of my brain, an absolute triumph of advertising.

Dumbstruck, I sent a brief email to my colleague, Shawna, a junior audio engineer based in North Hollywood. Shawna was barely thirty, a weekend DJ, originally from Albuquerque.

This is how old I am, I told her. *I actually remember this commercial from my childhood and can recite the entire thing, word-for-word.*

I included a link to the ad on YouTube.

Shawna responded, simply, with "hehehe"—what else was she supposed to say?—and as I went to close out the email, I noticed that her signature contained, as Millennial email signatures often do, a famous quotation of sorts, though this one was unattributed.

Nature loves courage, it said. *Hurl yourself into the void.*

Years ago, when Franny and I were still dating, we flew to Minneapolis, where she had been raised, and stayed with my future in-laws in the family home. Sitting on the couch that afternoon, shortly after arrival, I watched as my mother-in-law, Karen Kay, walked over and, without preamble, handed me my wife's retainer from when she was in high school, along with a plaster mold of her adolescent teeth. The intention here was humor, though it took me a second to catch on.

Karen Kay was a character of the quintessential Midwestern variety. Originally from Kansas. Had grown up on a mid-century dairy farm in the vast, open plains. No indoor plumbing. A move to Chicago for college and then on to Minnesota for marriage. A slightly zany and entirely dear woman, one of the easiest laughers I ever knew. Over the years, she had created her own language, a kind of baby-talk dialect rooted in the experiences of early motherhood, experiences to which she had formed a deep and lasting sense of attachment. Kleenexes, for example, were called "horn-blowers." Cookies were called "coo-coos." Snacks were called "snacky-poos." And so on. All with the Minnesota accent. It drove Franny absolutely nuts.

Enough with the baby talk, Mom, she would say.

But her mother was unstoppable. The baby talk never abated, and in fact it might well have intensified as she moved through her twilight years. Karen Kay had always referred to Franny by a small set of nicknames, each of which derived from the word *pumpkin* (pronounced "punkin"): Punker, Punky, Punk-a-dunk. And for more than four decades, she had clung with religious devotion to nearly every single artifact from her daughter's childhood, squirreling it all away in boxes, burying it down in the basement, for removal at a later date.

·

I reflect on this now by way of contrast, recognizing that throughout my life, including my time as a father, I have exhibited the exact opposite tendency, perhaps to an excessive degree. Rather than wanting to keep everything forever, I want to throw it all away as soon as possible. I don't care what it is. I want it gone. Nothing would make me happier. Get rid of it. The accumulation of stuff makes me anxious.

I don't even like the accumulation of hair, I sometimes joke. I'm the only guy in the world who wants to be bald.

·

As a film student in Boulder in the late '90s, my senior thesis film—my parting shot as an undergraduate—addressed these themes in rough detail. It was an experimental documentary of sorts, a slapdash effort assembled at the last minute under the heavy influence of weed. Much of it features me, alone, staring into the camera lens, describing an episode from the night before, when I had been studying for final exams but felt restless and so went into the bathroom and picked up some electric clippers and looked at myself in the mirror and decided to shave my head bald. I actually started to do it, too—the only time in my life that I'd ever acted on the impulse. But almost as soon as I began, I balked and chickened out, exiting the bathroom and returning to my books.

My presentation in the film is intentionally deadpan. I am baked out of my gourd. Making eye contact with my audience, I explain the minor hair episode, and at the end of the anecdote point to a solitary white patch on the left side of my head where the clippers had found their purchase.

It is then that the film jump-cuts for no discernible reason to some footage of a gorilla in a zoo. Classical music plays. I do a voice-over of sorts, a kind of improvised free verse poetry, attempting to channel what's going on in the gorilla's mind. All throughout the process, I keep bursting into fits of laughter.

And so on.

•

These were the kinds of disparate memories that

went through my head that afternoon in the garage, as I sat there editing Twinkie audio, reflecting on my departure from Twitter, meditating on my late mother-in-law and film school and the snack cake commercials of my youth. The weight of obsessive nostalgia and the reality of impermanence. Fear of attachment. My minimalist fantasies. Again I considered the little quotation in Shawna's email signature—*Hurl yourself into the void*—and noted to myself that I'd never *actually* shaved my head, not once in my life, not even for kicks, and probably never would, despite a stated desire to do so. My vanity wouldn't permit me. Fear of professional reprisal. Not that it really mattered much, in and of itself. But what *did* matter was this idea of follow-through. Feeling something deeply and then doing something about it. Finding myself in a moment of epiphany, however minor, and having the courage to move. I wanted to be this kind of person, bold, a man strongly attuned to his gut.

It was in this spirit—a kind of fever, really—that I decided, quite abruptly, the following morning, to sell my truck. Something else that I'd been meaning to do but had so far failed to actualize. For years, we'd had two cars in the driveway but really only needed one. I worked mostly from home, only occasionally on-site. When that happened, I could easily get around via Lyft, ride my bike, take the train. No problem. In the grand scheme of things, it would save us money. A no-brainer.

Not to mention, I told Franny, that it's good for the environment. I'll be able to look at our grandkids one day and tell them that I actually did something to save the world from climate change.

She made a face at me but conceded that the logic was fairly sound. A shrug of her shoulders. *Up to you.* I took it as a dare, and a few hours later, during my lunch break, I left the house and drove out to CarMax in Burbank, where, within a matter of minutes, I unloaded my 2001 Cherokee. A short bit of paperwork, a mechanic's evaluation, and it was done. A heavyset guy in a sport coat handed me a check. Another strong act of unburdening, and a surprisingly emotional one. For all of my professed love of simplicity, here I was, a grown man, a little choked up as I looked out at the Jeep for the last time, the Jeep that had taken me up and down the coast of California, out to the desert, into the hills. The Jeep in which Franny and I had gone out on our earliest dates. The Jeep in which I had driven the kids home from the hospital after their respective births. A whiff of Karen Kay nostalgia, overtaking me. *Bye-bye, Mr. Jeepers. So long.*

·

Feeling bereft, I exited CarMax and stepped into the midday sun, ordered a Lyft and was told to expect a fifteen-minute wait. Rather than stand there, grieving like a fool, I figured I would kill the time by walking across the street to a gas station, where I bought myself an iced tea and a Cliff Bar. As I stood in line at the register, I noticed the digital lottery board mounted on the wall. The Powerball jackpot, up to a whopping $900 million. I added a single ticket to my bill. Not uncommon behavior for me. Another contradiction in character. Both an anti-materialist and a man prone to playing the lottery, especially when the jackpots got massive. Never mind the fact that public lotteries were essentially regressive taxes levied on the poor. Never mind that the odds of winning were worse than, say, the odds of getting struck by lightning in the Mojave. I rationalized the activity as a kind of frivolous fun, a simple two-dollar lark, a way of maintaining a bit of excitement in life. After all, *what if?* Somebody had to get struck by lightning. Might as well be me.

As I sat in the back of my Lyft, headed home, I held the ticket in my hand and looked at the dot matrix numbers and fell into a detailed fantasy of my life and how I would conduct it, post-victory, a man worth nearly a billion dollars overnight. I saw Franny and I having a fevered conversation at the kitchen table. What to do. How to behave. The impact this would have on our kids, our relationships with family and friends. Our sense of self. Our feelings of purpose. We would tell no one, we decided, except for immediate family. There were attorneys and board rooms, a team of financial advisors, everybody required to sign an ironclad NDA. Inquiries into our identities by anyone in the media would be declined as a matter of course. We were private citizens and would like to remain so. End of story.

We will not let this destroy us, we said.

Most all of the money would be given away. The only proper response, the only way to prevent this obscene windfall from unleashing its corrupting forces. Anything less would be a gross injustice, a direct violation of core principles. But it was also important to give it away smartly. Maximize its value. Do the most good. Be wise.

I don't even like the accumulation of hair. The only guy in the world who wants to be bald.

In my fantasy, as in my senior thesis film, there was now a jump-cut, a sudden leaping forward to the days after my death, many years hence. Friends and colleagues, most of them up in age, commenting to reporters, talking into television cameras. The money never changed them, they said. We never even knew they had it, they said. A flurry of op-eds and profiles, heralding our decision to live modestly and give away our mega-fortune in complete anonymity.

There was then the incongruous thought of how fun it would be to take an utterly reckless approach with a certain percentage of the fortune. Twenty million dollars, for example, given away as randomly as possible, on an annual basis. A kind of performance art, a subversive act of philanthropy, the ridiculing of greed. I would move around the country in disguise. Big fistfuls of cash dropped on people's front porches. Ten grand handed to teenagers at drive-through windows. Walking up to homeless people in the streets, quietly placing duffle bags at their feet filled with crisp, $100 bills.

·

An abrupt stop at an intersection near the Hollywood Bowl snapped me out of the reverie. Lurching forward a bit, pressing against my seatbelt, I became aware of what I was up to, where my head had gone, how far the fantasy had taken me in a matter of moments. There was an embarrassed grin, accompanied by a clear sense of doom, an understanding that I absolutely *would not win this lottery now*, that nobody ever won the lottery who thought this much about winning the lottery. Without even realizing it, I'd fucked myself. Behavior like this was disqualifying. Miraculous luck never channeled itself into men who lusted after riches so grotesquely. The winner was always some random sixty-eight-year-old grandmother who bought a ticket as an afterthought, along with some Pringles and a carton of milk.

I could feel a faint ache in my chest as I imagined this woman with her winning ticket. The blue hair. The dumbstruck smile. Holding an oversized check on the front page of the local paper. Like a lucky orphan getting adopted, saved from a life of relative squalor, rocketed into the Daddy Warbucks stratosphere, no longer cursed with the burden of having to remember money. The dream of being able to forget.

It was here, with this vision playing in my head, that I reached for my phone and went to open Twitter, my longtime reflexive response to minor emotional discomfort, conditioned over more than ten years. But of course the app was nowhere to be found, vanquished from my home screen, functioning now as a kind of phantom limb.

Aware of what I'd done, I let out a quiet, defeated chuckle and stared out the window at the blur of Hollywood passing me by. The Capitol Records building. An abuela on the corner selling fruit. The events of the past twenty-four hours, coming into sharper focus. This relinquishment of old selves and old ways. A big purge. And in the midst of it, another small moment of personal idiocy, unfolding in the back of a smelly Lyft. Dreaming of millions, reaching like a zombie for my phone. This, I told myself, should be my métier, precisely the sort of thing I needed to be writing about in my book. These minor-key moments of fear and desire. These flurries of spasmodic change and absurd little fluctuations of mind. Quiet agonies. Ludicrous fantasies. My middle-aged motions toward austerity. No car, no clarity, no social media. No lottery winnings, either. And how palm trees had always looked like toilet brushes to me, reaching up to the filthy sky. Life in all of its splendor, right here. There was something to be said about all of it, and if I had any guts, I would say it. I would shut myself off from the world and concentrate long enough to get it down. Probably it wouldn't amount to much, but that was beside the point. And anyway, who knew? This was, after all, a world in which a man could make a fortune by inventing something as obnoxious as the Twinkie. To sit around predicting outcomes was a mostly futile exercise. And there was no holding on to anything, either. It was all going, it would all go, it was all gone. You could either be the gorilla in the cage at the zoo, or you could hurl yourself into the void.

MY NAME IS Brad—a fact I've given a lot of thought to over the years. Probably too much. The word itself means "broad wood" or "broad meadow." English in origin. In my lifetime it has become a cultural pejorative. Think of any movie or television show with a character named Brad in it. He's never good news. It's an absolute fact. There have been studies done. It has something to do with the New England aristocracy of yore. The name's popularity peaked in the year 2000, when it was the 632nd most common baby name for boys in the United States. Since then its usage had faded.

.

A while back, I talked with an author named Brad Phillips for my podcast. A heavily tattooed, laconic Canadian, brilliant and quick, with a fondness for drugs. Fluent in Buddhism. Also a gifted painter. He was, among the hundreds of episodes I've recorded over the years, the very first writer named Brad to guest on the show.

Together we lamented our shared name.

Two Brads equal one Dwayne, he told me.

•

Who am I? A question I often ask myself.

Also: *What happened? And what should I do? And why am I here?*

The problem of how to be a person.

The issue of what to write down.

•

I was born in a hospital in Milwaukee. In the moments after being born, I peed in the doctor's face. He pulled me out of the birth canal, headfirst into daylight, and in response I peed on him. First thing I ever did on this earth. This is what my mother has always told me. This is what I usually tell people when the subject of my birth comes up—as if it were an act of defiance, like I was actually *aiming* at the guy, arrived on planet Earth with incredible comic timing—when the truth is that I was terrified and lost bladder control in front of strangers while weeping.

•

My maternal great-grandfather was, according to family lore, a musical prodigy, a wizard on multiple instruments, the piano in particular. Yet as a child, I was never given piano lessons. No exposure. Neither of my parents had the gift. *But what,* I sometimes wonder, *if I do? What if this ability has been passed down to me, unbeknownst to me? What if I've been wandering through my days, oblivious to my inheritance, tragically out of sync with my own wiring?*

I could always take a piano lesson, of course—it's never too late—but at this point I'm almost afraid to try. Afraid that I might uncover the latent gift, the ability to play by ear with my eyes closed, a reckoning that would force me into a painful confrontation with my un-lived life as a rock star.

I'm a writer, I tell myself, by way of consolation. Words are a kind of music, too. A keyboard is a keyboard—right?

And it's not like I grew up in a cloistered environment. I had a record collection as a child, a stereo in my bedroom. Played in the school band in the fourth and fifth grades. Percussion. Typical boy move. Given a choice of instruments, and I opted for the drums. What did I want to do? I wanted to beat on something. And exhibited no particular talent for it, either. A passable sense of rhythm at best. My interest was minimal, and

I distinguished myself not at all. And then it was over, and I never went back.

And the reason I never went back, I tell myself, is because I don't have the gift, full stop. Musical talent being on par with something like athletic prowess. Height, weight, agility, speed. Perfect pitch. Manual dexterity. Either it's there or it's not. And if you have it, you almost certainly know about it. The kind of shine that announces itself plainly at a young age. The purest forms of ability and their irrepressible nature, abilities that arrive whole and pristine, in a swirl of DNA. The kind that cause people to thank God in public and walk around feeling special about themselves, as well they should.

That I have been blessed in this lifetime with no such bounty puts me in league with the mass of humanity. The small consolation of numbers. All of us out here in the earthly wilderness, banging on our little drums in fits of arrhythmia, unable to play with the angels.

·

From one of my notebooks:

If you want your book to be enjoyable it's gonna need some narrative. It needs characters moving in space. Moments of domestic bliss. Family comedy to leaven the baseline tragedies.

*Things like Oscar asking me to make him a
pasta smoothie, which he actually did the other
day.* Daddy, can I have a pasta smoothie? *And
dammit, I should've made him one. I regret
so much that I didn't. I laughed and kissed
the crown of his head, but I didn't make the
goddamned smoothie. Precisely the sort of
miniature failing that, with accumulation over
time, morphs into a giant ball of regret. And
this is what I'm gonna choke on in the moment
of my passing from this earth. A final, tortured
haunting as the lights go down. Not in-the-
moment enough. Not enough spirit. Not enough
fun or appreciation. It all goes fast. And then it's
gone. And there you were. Just put the fucking
noodles in the blender, you fascist.*

•

You should write a funny novel, my friend Penny once
told me.

We were walking down the street together. I was
telling her about my book, some version of it, and how
it was driving me completely insane.

You're funny, she said. Have some fun with it.
Write something funny.

I'm trying, I said. But it always comes back to
what's heavy. Death and grief and tragedy and all the

rest. It's like I can't avoid it. But somehow there has to be jokes.

Humor, she said, and I'm paraphrasing, is emotional pain remembered in a state of complete serenity.

It's the second part, I said, that's causing me all the problems.

Okay, said Penny. Then here's another approach: Instead of being funny, pay careful attention to the things you're most ashamed of, and put all of *those* things in the book.

•

Okay then.

I'm ashamed of the fact that I once peed on my neighbor's dog. (Again I'm peeing on someone—a disturbing trend.) I was six, maybe seven years old. My buddy, Nathan, egging me on. This poor old black lab in a chain-link enclosure on the side of a pale yellow house. And how the woman who owned the dog was standing inside and caught the tail end of the cruelty from her kitchen window. She picked up the phone and dialed my mother, who took me by the arm and marched me over to the woman's front door and made me apologize in person—the most vivid part of the experience. The heat of the guilt and how it never fully leaves you. Standing on that porch with my head down. *I'm sorry I peed on your dog.*

•

I'm ashamed of the fact that I suicidally ideate, but only rarely, in moments of deepest frustration, and not, I hope, in any kind of serious way. It's more like Wile E. Coyote-style, me out in the desert with dynamite strapped to my chest, giving two middle fingers to the sun. Always with an element of bleakest humor.

I can, for example, get intensely frustrated with the requirements of professional adulthood, the grinding insanity of it all. How everybody's always trying to do stuff and accomplish things, and get somewhere, and go someplace, and be someone, and win and not lose. In moments of particular overwhelm, it can make me want to go to the beach and run very fast across the sand, straight into the ocean, and swim until I can't swim anymore and then sink to the bottom of the ocean with both of my middle fingers once again extended heavenward. But of course I'm not going to *actually* do that. I'm not going to *literally* run to the bottom of the ocean. I'm going to remain on the shore, and I'm going to watch the waves crash on the shore and I'm going to watch the children play in the waves, as debris from a faraway nuclear power plant washes onto the sand.

But then the very next day—and this is where things can get muddled—it's entirely possible that I might wake up and experience feelings of shame around what I believe to be my lack of proper ambition. The worrying absence of laser focus and raging competitive fire. The itinerant nature of my career, bouncing around from thing to thing, trying on different roles, forever experimenting, doing "just fine" but never fully distinguishing myself in any particular discipline. *Is this some kind of moral failure?* I might ask myself. *Am I wasting my chance to make a difference, or am I simply a man of diversified interests?* My standards seem reasonably high and my work ethic has always been strong—certainly nothing to be "ashamed of," per se. And yet the shame in certain moments is undeniably there, usually accompanied by feelings of deepest fatigue. Dreaming of stillness in a culture that celebrates hyperactivity. Everybody always conflating their sense of self with their professional pursuits. Everybody always telling everybody else how fucking busy they are. It's so exhausting.

·

I was fired from a burrito restaurant when I was in college. A little bit of shame here, too. The manager and I got into a verbal altercation at around 1:00 AM, shortly after I finished cleaning the deep fryer. The next day, when I reported to work, I was asked to hand in my apron. I feel bad about it still.

·

There was, too, the time I was working for a tech startup, years ago. A sales job, of all things, a job laughably at odds with my fundamental nature, one that required me to suppress, rather than express, my encompassing sense of doubt. A lot of tension in that office environment, as I recall. Gold rush mentality, pure American and desperate. Startups tend to be desperate places. I was a mediocre salesman at best. What I did amounted to cold-calling eight hours a day. That or I dicked around on the internet. Then it ended.

It was a Friday morning, first thing, when I was called into a meeting with the company's chief operating officer—a large, ruddy, Southern man who had, it was known, thrown the shot put in college. We met in the conference room. He rose to his feet when I entered. A strong handshake. We sat down. There was amiable small talk for about thirty seconds before his expression flatlined, the light draining out of his eyes. He calmly explained, in his Mississippi drawl, that the purpose of our meeting was unpleasant and that my employment, effective immediately, had been terminated. There would be no severance. My health insurance would expire in two weeks. My last paycheck would be sent in the mail. He wished me luck.

I thanked him, rose from my chair, exited the room and walked downstairs, aware of my swirling emotions—relief most prominently, but also there was sadness, shame, humiliation, dread. Arriving in the bullpen, I announced to my coworkers, perhaps a bit too loudly, that I'd been canned. Apparently by then the word had spread: it was a mass execution. All of us, save four executives, were gone. The company was effectively dead.

Reactions varied. Margot, the sales director, turned red in the face and kept saying *What?* repeatedly. Lori, the admin assistant, went silent and stared at her hands. Dan, the handsome Kiwi, who had once been a male model, got emotional. I guess this means I go back to Christchurch, he said, his voice catching. Almost everyone, myself included, told him he'd be better off.

I did a quick lap, shaking a few hands, saying some quiet goodbyes, then went home. These were my bachelor days. A small studio apartment in Silver Lake. I stood in the kitchenette, reading the paper, eating handfuls of peanuts, then put on some sweatpants and climbed into bed. Messaging my friend Summer, I broke the news that I'd just been laid off, that the company had fully imploded. She asked what I planned to do next.

I think, I said, with more bitterness than I had previously allowed, *I'm going to do absolutely nothing as often as possible until I die.*

I then texted my friend Paul, a classmate from college who now lived in China, teaching English. I told him I had lost my job and had very little interest in finding another one. He advised that if I didn't like capitalism, I should focus on studying aboriginal cultures and emulate how they lived, ate, and related to their natural environments.

·

More recently, there had been the ill-fated job I'd had producing documentary television for a company that must, for legal reasons, go unnamed. What I can safely say is that the project required me to fly across the country and spend a few days in the presence of a billionaire, about whom we were making a flattering, multi-episode profile.

It was, to date, the first and only time in my life that I've ever had close proximity to a billionaire. What I remember most about him is not the man himself—a nice enough fellow, possessed of a bland affect, exhibiting exactly the kind of aloof self-assuredness and air of entitlement that one might expect from someone who hadn't pumped his own gas in thirty years. What struck me most instead was the coterie of assistants with whom he traveled at all times, a quartet of junior executives who functioned as his brain trust, a kind of elaborate human shield, tending to his every thought and need, and quietly, ferociously, competing with one another for his favor. It was in the harsh dynamics of their subterranean combat that I felt the truth of the billionaire, the ways in which power and money have a tendency to make people nuts. The gravitational force of this one man's good fortune, bending everything it came into contact with. A winning lottery ticket in human form. So tantalizingly close. So impossibly far.

All told, I spent about twelve hours in the billionaire's company over a span of three days— an amount of time, the junior executives repeatedly informed me, *that no one ever gets*. The billionaire's time was simply too valuable. He didn't need to do things like this. He didn't need to do anything except for what he wanted to do, obviously. The fact that he wanted to do this was extraordinary. Repeatedly, I assured them of how appreciative I was, trying not to let their exhortations mess with my head. In my role as lead producer, it was my responsibility to stay cool, be unbothered, keep the trains running on time, and never seem cowed by anything. I liaised with the billionaire in his dressing room, making sure he felt comfortable with the day's agenda, and then, when filming began, I sat behind the camera and conducted the interview, pitching him softball questions about his life and career, questions intended to elicit the kinds of responses that would lead to quality, inspiring television. His mother's love. His father's absence. The teachers who believed in him. The Ivy League scholarship. The influential mentor. The early career failures and moments of doubt. The eventual breakthrough, followed by the obligatory crash. The late-thirties coronary scare. The remarkable comeback and incredible series of triumphs. A commercial for the greatness of the man.

In this spirit, it should have been a relatively straightforward production, tracing the glittering contours of his Wikipedia profile. But what I didn't know, and could not possibly have known at the time, was that the billionaire harbored political ambitions, had grown restless in quasi-retirement, had secretly launched an exploratory committee and was pondering a run for high office. Over the course of the three-day interview process, he repeatedly, out of nowhere, in the midst of my questioning, went off-script, turning his gaze to the camera lens, delivering excerpts from a generic stump speech, jabbing his closed fist for emphasis like a seasoned pro. In the absence of any context, these non sequiturs made little sense to me, so much so that I wondered if it might be a sign of senility, some pitiful delusions of grandeur spilling forth. Over and over again, I gently reminded the billionaire to please redirect his focus, requests that he repeatedly ignored, as if he hadn't heard them at all. By the end of day one, it was clear that a hostile takeover was underway. The billionaire was now in charge of the production. Events would unfold on his terms, as events almost always did.

.

Back in Los Angeles, company executives were, to put it mildly, displeased, as confused as I was by the billionaire's behavior, his fixation on politics, his need to wax rhapsodic about the spirit of the American people and the promise of a better future. Most of all, though, they were upset with me for failing to bring him to heel and get the production back on track. I made efforts to explain how hard I had tried, how insane the exchanges had been, how I had even approached the quartet of junior executives during a bathroom break, pulling them into video village and pleading for some assistance. But of course no such assistance was forthcoming. Their only allegiance was to their king.

·

In the end, I was able to cut the show together, albeit a considerably shorter version than the one that we had planned. Six long weeks were spent on-site in an edit bay, sweating over every frame, enduring the quiet judgment, the gossip and consternation among my peers. When post-production wrapped shortly before Christmas, I said my goodbyes and exited the premises, aware that I would never be asked to work for the company again. I felt both ashamed of the failure and relieved to be free of the insanity. All throughout that holiday season, I slept like a bear. During daytime hours, I was both moody and rejuvenated, restless in my uncertainty about what would come next, and excited, in some vague way, about the possibilities. At the turn of the new year, I fell into the customary planning mode, giving thought to goals and priorities and how to build a viable future. In my notebook, I wrote the following:

I want to be one of those gentle, wise fathers who never raises his voice or has an unkind word to say, who is almost always in control, a stellar breadwinner, calm and good-natured, with free time to spare, loose and relaxed, fun, funny, uninhibited, both subversive and profitable, a man who books impromptu vacations and plans camping adventures and knows how to use power tools and participates willingly in school functions and is the envy of the other mothers. But instead here I am in my garage, contending with my inner life, Brad the Sad Dad, man of soft and complicated beliefs, the living embodiment of a collective mood?

•

The aforementioned passage was scribbled at my desk in the garage, the place where I now spent a majority of my time, and where, during the first six weeks of that year, I wrote a very mediocre screenplay, hammering it out in a panicky rush. The soul-sucking humorlessness of the billionaire project had left its mark on me, and in response I decided to be silly, an attempt at alchemy. Working on a regular schedule, I cranked out at least five pages a day, a copy of *Save the Cat!* dog-eared on my desk. What I ended up with was an absurd comedy called *Man of Letters.*

It's like a sports comedy, I told Franny, but the sport is spoken word poetry.

A look of expectation on her face, as if she were waiting for the punch line.

In the fantastical world of the film, spoken word poetry is a major spectator sport, highly competitive, on par with, say, professional basketball. Our hero is a heartbroken forty-year-old poet who lives with his parents in a bland suburban hell. (Picture Will Ferrell with a wild head of hair and a massive hermit's beard.) A Salingeresque figure who was once a great champion but then vanished without a trace, retreating into obscurity to tend his psychic wounds. As the movie unfolds, he emerges from reclusion and begins to live again, slowly reentering the realm of competition, eventually defeating his longtime arch-rival for the championship. Along the way he falls in love with a registered nurse.

I've lived my life, he says in the climactic poetry competition—

. . . up here onstage,
pacing like a panther and
articulating rage.
Working like a demon
for a paltry living wage.
Rattling the bars of
this unholy cosmic cage.

My literary agent, in an act of compassion, helped me find a film agent to shop the project around—a British guy, about my age, based in Santa Monica. He used the word "bespoke" too much. We met only once in person. That was plenty. The rest happened over the phone. A fairly rapid rejection process, embarrassing for all parties. The script, the Brit assured me, had made it all the way into the hands of Will Ferrell's longtime manager, who, while "charmed" by my ability to write poetry, ultimately found the project "too quirky to pursue"—a sentiment that was echoed by pretty much everyone who read it, assuming they even did.

·

In the aftermath of this small debacle, I quickly fell back into production work, scrounging up a pair of small jobs in rapid succession, including, for the first time, an audio production job, which I lied my way into by claiming that I knew how to use Pro Tools. That I was able to fake my way through the project was the principal source of my self-esteem that spring. Teaching myself the software basics in quick turnaround, hustling, watching YouTube tutorials, sourcing all necessary gear, setting up a little studio in a corner of the garage, complete with a mixing board and a pair of microphones. The project itself was of little interest: educational content for a real estate concern, all about how to flip homes. The drabness of the subject matter notwithstanding, there was something energizing about the feat—the thrill of a scam, successfully executed. And along with it a bit of uneasiness born of disorientation. The good with the bad. The highs and the lows. The summit of Mt. Everest had once been the seafloor.

.

It was toward the end of this project, early on a Monday morning, that I sat down at my desk to work and heard my phone ring. Not even 8:00 AM. Unusual. My father on the other end of the line, calling with the devastating news that my buddy, Pete, had died. One of my oldest and dearest friends from childhood. As close to a brother as I would ever have in this world. The news had gotten to my parents first, via Facebook, and my dad was calling to let me know. The conversation lasted all of a minute, my old man lowering the boom in his just-the-facts manner. *Found dead this morning. At a bachelor party in Key West. Died in his sleep. A friend discovered his body. Unclear on cause at this point. Still waiting for word. I'm so terribly sorry to have to tell you this, son.* There wasn't much else to say. I was so shocked, I could barely respond. I hung up and stood there for a long moment, blinking, then went inside and explained to Franny what had happened, blurting it out in a single, painful line: *My buddy Pete just died.* She jumped up from her chair, her cheeks suddenly flushed, and gave me a hug.

After relaying what little I knew, I walked into the bathroom and looked at myself in the mirror and put a fist to my face, bursting into tears, working to hold them in, as if there were an animal trying to escape from my chest. Weird tears, in retrospect. An explosion of emotion, yes. But also a performance of grief.

I didn't know what else to do. My buddy Pete had died.

•

This is what happens, I kept telling myself all throughout that morning, as if I had struck upon a revelation. *This is normal. People die. People die every day. This is tragic, but people die every day.*

•

There were calls to make. Reaching out to old friends, breaking the awful news, commiserating. The terrible shock of it all. Coordinating travel plans. I booked a flight to Boston for the coming Thursday, then decided to go for a hike and burn off some energy and get some air, be in contact with nature, try to clear my head. I left the house and walked up to Griffith Park, where, while making my ascent, I noticed a large black bird with a sizable wingspan circling in the skies above. In the fog of my grief I invested it with a kind of mystical symbology, convinced that the bird was a manifestation of Pete, that this was Pete saying goodbye, transitioning to the next realm, reincarnated instantly, and so on. *It's a hawk,* I told myself. *A beautiful, soaring, solitary hawk.*

But then on my flight to Boston that Thursday, sitting in a middle seat at the back of the aircraft, it occurred to me that it might have been a vulture.

•

Three days later, upon returning home from the funeral, I found myself in a state of considerable softness. That punch drunk feeling you get from deep grief, dizzying and clarifying all at once. The cause of death, almost certainly, was an accidental opiate overdose. The news had been relayed throughout the weekend, in quiet corners, in hushed tones, in weepy little semicircles of mourners. Some hidden pill bottles had been found among Pete's belongings at home, just as one was discovered in his dopp kit in Key West. An autopsy had been performed. Toxicology results pending. The basic facts seemed clear enough. Pete, away at a bachelor party, had called his wife and daughters to tell them goodnight. Nodded off in bed and was found there, dead, by a friend the following morning. Just a sickening tragedy. His widow, Meredith, a Boston native, so utterly devastated. She hadn't seen it coming at all.

•

If there was anything positive about the experience, it was the fact that the long weekend had amounted to a high school reunion of sorts. Some of my closest friends and I, gathered together for the first time in ages. We had all grown up in suburban Milwaukee, and in the decades since almost everyone had fled, scattering across the country, building families, chasing dollars. To have everyone in the same room was a rare occurrence. It felt good. The easy familiarity and irreplaceable shorthand. We drank ourselves silly in the hotel bar and told old stories and blamed ourselves for not keeping in better touch, for not reaching out to Pete enough, for getting too distracted by the bullshit, for not knowing what the hell was actually going on with anyone. There were drunken vows to get together on an annual basis going forward, ski trips and beach vacations, and so on—vows that would never be kept. We were determined, we told ourselves, to get our priorities in order.

All of it amounted, I think, to a collective expression of shame, and an admission of how alienating modern life could be. The wicked loneliness that so often characterized adulthood, the majority of social exchanges relegated to the digital realm. The avalanche of responsibilities bearing down—financial, parental, and otherwise—taxing vital energies, making friendships hard to maintain, especially those carried out over distances. In lieu of an actual conversation, you might fav an Instagram post or send a photo via text. How easy it was to trick yourself into thinking you were actually keeping in touch with people, when all you were really doing was scratching the surface.

And then, before you knew it, they were gone.

•

It was just a few weeks after the funeral that I launched, on a whim, the *Otherppl* podcast. Late summer, 2011. A direct expression of my grief and shame, and the resulting experimental mood. The basic concept was simple: in-depth conversations with other people— other writers. No rote journalistic approach or stacked list of questions. We would just talk and see what happened, personal and off-the-cuff, in keeping with the tenets of podcasting. No high-minded literary discussions or synopsizing of a book. Nothing too polished or produced or removed from the messiness of the real. My first guest was Jonathan Evison, an old writer friend from Seattle. We had known one another for years and had published our first novels at around the same time. I talked with him over Skype and recorded it with my new gear. He was in his RV, which he used as a roving office.

You're sequestered in your mobile home? I said.

Yeah, he said. Are we rolling or something?

Yeah. I've got Jonathan Evison on the line.

Let me put some pants on, he said.

At the time, I had no idea that I was embarking on a project that would carry me through a decade and beyond. I think I figured I would conduct the experiment, make a couple dozen shows, get it out of my system, and move on to something else. But right away, the exchanges felt good—medicinal, even. And what feedback I received was all positive. There was something undeniably energizing about it, something natural and fun, a kind of necessary corrective to the general trend. The wonderful mess of an uncut conversation vs. a sculpted, pithy tweet.

Hosting the show came pretty easily to me, but the truth is that it's an easy thing to do. Nothing complicated. Just sit there and pay attention. Try to serve as a surrogate for the audience at home. Have a little courage and accept the risk of boredom. Certainly it was easier than writing a book, which was part of the appeal. It felt like an act of service, a kind of community-building exercise, a reaching out to the weary hordes of literary geeks on the periphery. In the beginning, I didn't spend too much time analyzing it. I just went with my instincts and followed what felt good.

.

In the decade since, over hundreds of episodes, there have been many small moments in which my guest and I have connected at an unusual level of depth, moments in which a deep forgetting seems to take place, a narrowing of attention and the removal of the usual divides. The static recedes, and what remains feels essential and true, a kind of mercy. It could be a funny story. It could be the revelation of tragedy or the sharing of a terrible humiliation. It could be just about anything. The only critical ingredient is transparency, the willingness to face things openly in the company of another person. On a functional level it can feel like an active demonstration of what it means to be human. When this happens, things get effortless and affirming in a hurry, occasionally even transcendent. The basic, deep relief of truly communicating with another human being, giving the mind its proper exercise, and silencing the voice in my head.

.

Along with writing, podcasting is the only thing I've ever done in my professional life that feels like any kind of fit. That both are esoteric, outsider pursuits is not at all lost on me. My other various day jobs, each of which has carried within it some vague notion of respectability and conventional prosperity, have always felt like a kind of play acting. The scramble for survival and the trying on of various selves. Yes, there have been some successes here and there, a certain kind of admirable industriousness at work. But generally these pursuits have felt devoid of any deeper meaning. The game, I've always told myself, is to somehow get back to the writing. It can be easy to worry that I've spread myself too thin, wandering down paths that have nothing at all to do with who I'm actually supposed to become.

The un-lived life of a parent, I once told Franny, can have enormous psychological impacts on a child. I read about it online. We think we're keeping secrets from them. They know everything.

We're screwed, she said.

Our job, I said, or one of our jobs, I think, is to

figure out what we're called to do. And then do what we're called to do.

So what are you called to do? she said.

I'm called to articulate my confusion, I said.

.

From one of my notebooks:

I feel like if we're poor, but I leave behind a stack of books, the kids will be proud of me, despite their suffering. They'll know that I suffered too but will hopefully find solace in the idea that at least I had someplace to put it all. He suffered richly, *they might say. Or, if we're fabulously wealthy and I leave behind a stack of bestsellers, they'll consider me a tremendous success and a man in full. They might even resent me for it. Or, if we're rich because I work some awful job that I hate, they'll be proud of me for my selflessness.* He sacrificed his dreams so that we might realize our own. *But if we're poor* and *I spend my life working a series of miserable jobs that I hate? In that case, they'll stand over my grave one day and say things like,* The old man was a tragic figure who wasted his one precious life on stupid bullshit.

A STORY I'VE been telling myself for a long time is that my identity has been shaped by the tragedies I've been witness to, and suffered through. The untimely deaths in particular. There have been too many of those. Accidents, illnesses, suicides. And of course Oscar's health challenges.

The doctors have informed us that there may also be some cognitive difficulties, though they can't say for sure at this juncture.

He's partially paralyzed on his left side.

.

Other stories I tell myself:

We tried too hard. We didn't listen to Nature. We didn't have enough money for IVF. Or maybe we did, but we were too damn stupid and cheap.

.

Your fundamental duty as a parent: protect your kids.

.

And maybe it was my sperm. Maybe my junk is messed up. Maybe there's something wrong with my dick. Of course you're going to think about this sort of thing. Most men's sperm are misshapen these days, according to reports. Two heads. Two tails. Insufficient swimmers. Mutations caused by endocrine disruptors. Chemical pesticides. Plastic containers in the microwave. The memory foam in your college mattress. The entire world, ready to poison you. Or maybe it was purely the egg. Maybe the egg was to blame. Maybe it was Franny's machinery and not mine. I guess I prefer to think of it as some combination, which of course it ultimately was. And anyway, we'll never know for sure. And even if we could know, which probably we can, we wouldn't want to know. Because what good would it do, other than lay one of us to waste?

.

The truth is that I could spend the rest of my life litigating the past, retracing steps, replaying events, building little narratives that amount, in the end, to "our fate." My conscience has always been prone to some heaviness. I can feel guilty about almost anything—the essential byproduct of a Catholic youth. Certainly I've made my share of mistakes. But where, I can't help but wonder, do the limits of a person's responsibility lie? How much of what we do or don't do in life should we be penalized for? When even the smallest, most innocent miscues can lead to such heartbreaking consequences. The brutal math of it all. Life and its many sucker punches. Stick around long enough, and you're bound to get your bell rung. Tragedy will eventually come calling for you—but not until you're fully unprepared.

•

Over the years I've framed the story to myself in any number of ways. I've told myself that Oscar is the culmination of something, a crescendo that my life had been building toward. That he is a matter of destiny, my destiny, a kind of spiritual test for which I have been chosen. That everything else that happened along the way had been in preparation for it—for this test, this responsibility, this kind of fatherhood. Both a pulverizing heartbreak and the honor of a lifetime. The infinite pain of it. The incalculable blessing.

Or, in my more severe and self-flagellating moods, I might see it as pure karmic punishment, a tragedy of my own creation, human suffering born of my own greed and foolishness. A harm that I created because I wanted too damn much, because I didn't think things through properly. A harm that I will one day be held accountable for, both by Oscar and by whatever gods might await me at the end of some tunnel of light.

We are our choices, I might tell myself. But we're not necessarily in control of them. The complicated issue of free will, which can leave me feeling unmoored. But then we're always unmoored. When are we ever tethered to anything? To be alive is to be in free fall. Never mind appearances. No stable shoreline or ground beneath our feet—though of course we like to pretend otherwise. The job here, I think, is to accept the fall. Relinquish all prideful illusions, confront the ambiguity of experience, and do the hard work of turning grief into laughter.

·

Not too long ago, Franny was tucking Oscar in, reading him a picture book called *I Broke My Trunk.* It's about an elephant named Gerald who slips and falls and breaks his trunk and tells his best friend, Piggie, about it. In the middle of the story, out of nowhere, Oscar looked up at Franny and asked her who broke his left arm.

How come it won't work? he wanted to know.

Four years old and wondering. It was bound to

happen sooner or later.

Franny told him no one broke his arm. That his arm was just made that way.

He looked at the arm for a long moment, rubbed it with his right hand, and gave the left elbow a kiss. Then he went back to the book.

Franny held it together. Finished reading. As the story came to its conclusion, I entered the room and took over, oblivious to the contents of their exchange. No detectable sadness in the air. Franny, with her Minnesota-Scandinavian roots, elite at the art of repression. Trading places with her, I climbed into bed with Oscar and snuggled him to sleep, and when I exited his room a few minutes later and walked down the hall to our bedroom, I found Franny sobbing in the shower.

.

And probably, I tell myself, this sort of thing is par for the course. Life as the parent of a sickly or disabled child is rife with little moments like these. Miniature obliterations. Quiet moments of complete disbursement that nobody else ever sees. Everywhere you go, the sadness is with you, just beneath the skin, always burning. It never leaves. What you have to do is learn how to carry it. It's like learning to carry fire.

•

Friends of ours rarely ask about it anymore or check in to see how we're doing. A small handful do, every once in a while, but that's it. Most stay quiet or pretend that it didn't happen. Probably they don't even give it a second thought. I can't say that I blame them—or sometimes I do, but only in my lowest moments. For the most part, I'm able to see it in perspective. Life is crazy. What are people supposed to do? Everyone has their own heartaches. And anyway this kind of thing has a tendency to leave you speechless. It certainly leaves me speechless, much of the time.

•

And of course there are the happy moments, too. Thousands of them. Little jewels. The good outweighing the bad. The summer we took the kids up the coast for a week. The hotel near the ocean that we paid for with credit card points. The afternoon when Franny took Alice down to the water and I stayed behind with Oscar to nap. And how we both fell asleep, watching cartoons, and woke up just after five o'clock with the girls coming into the room.

How was the beach? I said.

Good, Alice told me. Kinda boring.

Why is that? I said.

It's always the same, she said. The rocks, the sand, the water.

I turned to Franny and said: My prodigy.

.

We fed the kids dinner in town that night and afterward went for some ice cream. Oscar in his braces, just beginning to take some steps. Alice holding his hand. Watching the two of them together. That alone. How happy Alice was to have her little brother up on his feet. Oscar too. The pride. The simple recognition of the goodness of it all. The toughness of my boy. The infinite patience of his big-hearted sister. Thinking of how much she did for him, quietly, daily, without complaint, adjusting to his rhythms, helping him stay upright.

It was hard for her, too.

.

When I tucked her in that night, I talked to her about it as we lay there in the dark, my head a little soft from the wine I'd had at dinner. I know you do a lot, I said. And I know that Oscar's situation isn't always easy for you. I know that you have to do things differently sometimes, and I just want you to know that I see it, and I'm very proud of you for being such a good big sister.

Her only response was: Thanks Daddy.

A bit of emotion in her voice. A bit of discomfort, too. Sentimental, half-drunk Dad and his heartfelt speeches. Still, I was glad that I'd said something. A rare moment in fatherhood when I felt like I'd gotten it halfway right.

·

In the year after Oscar's diagnoses, I had a recurring dream in which he would stand up and start to walk, tentatively at first, wobbling, before picking up speed and breaking into a flat-out sprint. My joy in these dreams was so powerful that it would always shock me awake. I'd lie there in the darkness, heart thudding, adjusting to the weight of reality, Franny snoring softly at my side.

There was the impulse to shake her and tell her what had happened, but I never did. Not at 3:00 AM. I couldn't bring myself to do it. Months would go by before I finally came clean, the dream repeating itself on a loop, an exquisite little torture, and then finally one morning I rolled over at daybreak and shared the news. Franny's eyes went wide. She told me that she'd been having the exact same dream.

·

Every fall there's a jog-a-thon at Alice's elementary school, invariably on the hottest day of the year, a four-hour slog on a Saturday morning, held to raise money for classroom supplies. One year, while Alice was off jogging with her friends, Franny and I walked Oscar around the track together. Oscar, back then, was in his little walker, moving at a snail's pace, taking frequent water breaks, surrounded by dozens of kids, every single one of them able-bodied, laughing and skipping and running free. The other parents stealing sad-eyed glances at us, sizing Oscar up, assessing his condition, wondering what exactly "went wrong." Franny and I with our eyes straight ahead. No choice other than to absorb the moment. Another such moment.

And then in the middle of it all, a little boy, maybe nine or ten years old, jogging past us, stopping abruptly and turning around, interrupting the spell of our grief. We'd never met this boy before. He knelt in front of Oscar, breathless, smiled and told him "good job, buddy" and gave him a high-five. Oscar beamed. The boy then stood up, looked us in the eye, and introduced himself as Ezra. An incredibly sweet and self-possessed child with caramel skin and bright hazel eyes. He told Oscar that he would stop and give him another high-five after the next lap. And then, before he turned and ran away, he looked directly at Franny and said with the utmost sincerity: I know it must be hard.

She burst into tears almost instantly. Her sunglasses hid it fairly well, but I could tell by her clenched expression that she was weeping. I got a little choked up, too, rubbing my eyes with the backs of my hands. In all the time since Oscar's diagnoses, it was easily the kindest and most intelligent thing anyone had ever said to us about it. A six-word line delivered from the mouth of a child, affirming our tiny reality.

WHEN ALICE WAS born, it went more or less according to script. Twenty-four hours of labor. Franny, opting for the epidural. The science fiction of vaginal delivery. My legs trembling wildly from adrenaline as I stood there, holding her hand. The sound of Alice's cries as the doctor pulled her into the world. The obnoxious thrill of it all. The obligatory photo. The cutting of the cord. Watching as she was weighed, poked, prodded, tested. Everything checking out fine. They cleaned her up and swaddled her. I stood over her, stupefied. She opened her eyes and looked up at me and blinked. I again took her picture. *Hi there, sweetheart. I'm your dad.* The bright pink skin. The alien eyes of a newborn, glassy and baffled and blue-black. Another picture. I remember thinking to myself: *She's fine.* And feeling terrified.

.

On the day that Oscar was born, I had a meeting with my old writing partner, Melissa, with whom I had sold a sitcom to MTV. We had been hoping to get a pilot order, but then the network announced an "executive reshuffling" and abruptly informed us that it would no longer be making scripted television. Our show was now dead. Nothing else to be done about it. If we wished to continue, we would have to start over from scratch and figure out what to do next, the prospect of which seemed unappealing.

I was on my way home from this meeting, feeling demoralized, when Franny called with the news that her water had broken. She was at The Grove, she said, a hellish outdoor shopping mall in West Hollywood. She and Alice had gotten a Wetzel's pretzel and sat down to eat it, and when she went to get up, the breakage occurred. The official term is "gross rupture." Cinematic. She was mortified. A mall employee had been kind enough to bring her a blanket, and she'd wrapped herself in it and waddled to the parking garage, leaking everywhere. Alice, age five, peppering her with questions the entire way.

.

A couple of hours later, Oscar was born via emergency C-section. We arrived in the maternity ward at Cedars and checked in, a little breathless, and within an hour it was done. A nerve-wracking flurry of activity. Some concern about the umbilical cord. The level of cervical dilation. Oscar's foot placement. Commiseration among doctors. Franny, rushed into surgery. Me, chasing after her, fumbling with my scrubs. The anesthesiologist. The lights. A countdown. The incision. The EKG, keeping time. The obstetrician, who seemed to appear from out of nowhere, rummaging around inside Franny's womb, blood everywhere. And then, as if by magic, there he was. My little man. Just like that. The doctor, holding him up like a trophy. *Here ya go, Dad. Take a picture.*

I took a picture.

•

Oscar didn't cry right away—the prevailing memory. And he was fairly limp in the doctor's hands, eyes closed. A surge of panic in my chest as I noticed this— but didn't say anything. There wasn't time. I snapped the photo, then followed as Oscar was whisked across the room to a little table in the corner where a team of doctors suctioned some fluid out of his lungs. And then came the cries. And I could breathe.

Nothing to worry about, one of the nurses assured

me. Fluid in the lungs is common with Cesareans.

The Dalai Lama, I later reminded myself, was silent when he was born. I had read that somewhere once. *He's just like the Dalai Lama.*

.

And that, really, was the extent of it insofar as hospital drama was concerned. No other indications of trouble. According to the obstetrician, we'd had a perfectly healthy baby boy. Franny had done beautifully in surgery. All stitched up and making progress. And Oscar was checking out fine. No red flags. Vitals were good. APGAR scores weren't elite, but were within the normal range. He'd emerged from the womb intact.

After five miscarriages and all of the attendant heartache, we had our second child. We had brought him into the world, as parents do, in an irrational act of love. The global ecosystem was in peril, and America, still recovering from the Great Recession, had seen its better days. My fledgling career as a television writer had just been derailed, and money would soon be a problem, as money often was. But even so, here we were, blissful and exhausted in the maternity ward, obedient to our biology, having made the decision to live inside our hopes instead of our fears, telling ourselves that somehow we would find a way.

•

I once had a great conversation with the author Lynne Tillman for the *Otherppl* podcast. One of my favorite guests of all-time. A New Yorker by way of Long Island. Wide open. Warm. The kind of person with whom you can discuss just about anything within five minutes of meeting her. After the interview wrapped, we sat around talking, off the record. I didn't want her to leave. She asked about my kids and seemed genuinely interested. I told her about Alice, my anxious eldest, fixated on death already. A teacher at her elementary school had recently told the story of Cesar Chavez, and somehow it had been communicated that Chavez had died in his sleep. Now Alice was terrified that she, too, would die in her sleep. We had been having trouble getting her to bed at night. The poor child, afraid to close her eyes. And almost certainly, I theorized, some of this anxious temperament had to be tied to Oscar's condition. Trying to process her little brother's malady. I could only speculate what it was doing to her. Deeper empathy, hopefully. Heightened awareness of fragility. The painful understanding that a body could be broken.

It can be hard, I said, coming to grips with their vulnerabilities. And then this world that we're sending them into. The insanity of it all. I can't help but wonder sometimes about the wisdom of procreation. Have I made a horribly misguided decision here? Do I owe these little people an apology?

There was some laughter, the dark kind. Lynne, quoting one of her favorite philosophers: *Optimism of the will; pessimism of the intellect.* We talked about lying. The odd necessity of it. A certain strain, anyway. The implicit dishonesties in any deep human relationship. Lying when you propose to your partner and tell her that the future will be rosy. Lying when you conceive a child, telling yourselves that everything will turn out just fine. And maybe, hopefully, for a certain period, it *will* be fine. But eventually, of course, as the years pile up, it gets grim.

•

And again, I'm not even sure if choice has all that much to do with it. We do what we do. The basic fact of our programming. Most of us wired to copy ourselves, perpetuating the cycles of existence. The old Samuel Beckett line about women giving birth astride a grave. Animals doing our animal business. A certain element of folly to it. A crushing kind of hopefulness, too. Bringing new life into the world at this particular moment in history. What beautiful fools we are. Babies born against a backdrop of escalating self-destruction. The miserable crime of climate change as their inheritance. The world and its many charades. Most everyone going through the motions, still pretending that carbon-fueled capitalism is somehow sustainable. Everyone caught in the riptide of it, unclear on how to escape. An economic model that operates according to the logic of a cancer cell. What we need is massive contraction, and what the system demands is endless growth. At some point, a tension that will resolve itself. We'll either change our ways radically, and soon, or the planet, it seems, will do away with us.

At times, I can find myself feeling resigned to it. A weary shrug. The Anthropocene devolving into an era of clarifying awfulness. Humanity forced into the evolutionary crucible. The earth's immune system, set into motion, culling the human population down to a more tolerable number. Sorry, kids. At best, a few million of us left behind on a mostly barren planet, windswept and scorched, the prophecies of Burning Man made manifest, a kind of primordial desert tableau.

Buzzards. Bartering. Bacchanals. A return to tribal society.

·

Or maybe we'll escape, I tell myself. Maybe space travel is the answer, though it can be hard to see exactly how. Whenever I try to think about the impossible enormity of the universe, what strikes me most is how pretty much all of it is designed to murder us. Mars, the leading candidate for colonization, with zero surface water or plant life, and equatorial temperatures averaging about 100 degrees below zero in summer. Not exactly Arcadia. And yet on some level I can understand the urge to go there. To look up into the heavens and *not* see a human future feels like a gross failure of the imagination, a kind of pitiful surrender. Better, I tell myself, as a general rule, to move in the direction of awe.

•

There's an asteroid called Apophis, I tell Franny. Named after the Egyptian god of death. I was reading about it in *National Geographic*. It's gonna buzz past Earth in 2029, and if it gets close enough, and moves through something called "the keyhole," then we're guaranteed a direct hit in 2036.

Perfect, she says.

The entire west coast of North America will be obliterated, I say. But only if it goes through the keyhole. If it misses the keyhole, we're fine.

Keep me posted, she says.

•

And how better, really, to respond to this kind of

100

information? The absorption of dire news about which nothing can be done—one of the defining characteristics of the modern age. At a certain point, it begins to feel like scenery. Stories of dread and destruction, rolling in like waves. A white noise backdrop against which everyday life unfolds.

To be in love with the world is, in the end, to be in a state of sadness over it. One and the same. Bad news encroaching from every direction. Good news on occasion as well. Human beings, caught in the crossfire, most of us in flight from ourselves, numb from all the forecasts, clutching at our smartphones, armed with our limited knowledge. Dancing anyway. Fucking anyway. Plotting and planning anyway. Flowers blooming anyway. Beautiful sunsets anyway. An assortment of possible futures, none of which is all that appealing. To avoid the worst, the experts tell us, we'll have to summon the best of ourselves. No pressure. Despair is a proportionate response, but to indulge in it would be immoral. The mess that we're in is unmistakable, and every single bit of it is a miracle. The irrepressible churn of life amid the slow-motion collapse. Selah. Relationships consummated. Babies wailing. Parents shouldering the responsibilities of parenthood, with all of its joys and terrors and labors and deep rewards, the endless logistics and constant improvisations. The growing acidity of the oceans. Glacial ice in rapid retreat. To be responsible for a human life in this kind of hothouse insanity. To bring a person into this world without even consulting her first. *Welcome to the accident, kid.* At times it can leave me feeling like I weigh a thousand pounds.

And yet for all my devotion to cold-eyed realism and hard prognostication, I can still find myself susceptible to sentimental moods. The melancholic longing for permanence, a heightened sensitivity to the speed of it all. Looking to the past, astonished by how much of my life is already gone. Just a handful of childhood memories left. Bits and pieces. The college years, an absolute blur. Early adulthood, a vapor. It goes. And now here I am, lost in the thick of middle age, my children still young, the planet going to absolute shit, and I know for a fact that I'll never see it clearly enough, no matter how hard I try. The very heart of my life, the golden age, the best of it, holy despite the darkness. And I'm missing it. Because I can't help but miss it. Because this is what human beings do: we miss things—even the best of things. We miss it and then we miss it. It's in front of us, and we can't see it. And then we lose it. And there it is.

IN GRADUATE SCHOOL at the University of Southern California, I took a fiction seminar with Hubert Selby, Jr., author of *Last Exit to Brooklyn, Requiem for a Dream*, and several other wonderfully profane meditations on the American underworld. Selby—or "Cubby," as everybody called him—was in his final days then. He would arrive in the classroom wheeling an oxygen tank behind him. Tubes in his nose. He had contracted tuberculosis as a young man while serving in the Merchant Marines and had battled severe pulmonary issues throughout his adult life. I studied with him in the spring of 2003. He died a year later, age seventy-five. A public memorial was held at the Egyptian Theater on Hollywood Boulevard. Well-attended. I showed up alone and sat toward the back, listening as friends and colleagues eulogized him, roasted him, and read aloud from his work. Toward the end of the ceremony, it was revealed that his final written words had been discovered on a sheet of paper at home. They went as follows:

A list of indignities:
Birth.
Death.

Witty to the end—a sinister wit. Perhaps more than anything, this is what impressed me most about him. A skeletal presence, barely able to breathe, showing up to class every week with an unlikely swagger, laughing at every joke, wheezing as he laughed, telling some good ones too, a man for whom life had clearly been hard, who had struggled through money troubles, battled with addiction, spent time in prison, married and divorced, raised his kids, taught himself how to write books. That he had taken his fair share of punches was clear just by looking at him. That he had fucked things up enormously on occasion was something to which he freely confessed. And yet here he was, still on his feet, a pile of novels to show for it, sober, mostly sane, working right up to the end, sense of humor intact. Against considerable odds, he had made a meaningful life for himself. He never quit. The central lesson. It would later be revealed that he had refused morphine on his deathbed despite some serious pain. Entirely in-character.

•

Another Cubby memory that stays with me: the time he informed me that I was a frustrated preacher. We were talking after class, discussing my latest workshop offering, a pitifully bad short story based on Aunt Rosalyn, my dad's older sister, who had died tragically in a drunk driving accident twelve years before I was born. From the detritus of this effort, Cubby was able to glean my obvious spiritual concerns, my misgivings about organized religion, my preoccupation with death, and my writerly inability to ever feel certain about anything. Yet at the same time there was the urgent need to get it all down on paper and make some kind of show of it.

Frustrated preacher, he said to me in his Brooklyn accent, tapping at my pages. I wrote entire books before I figured it out. Takes one to know one, man. I've been a frustrated preacher my whole life.

A generous moment of commiseration and in retrospect a keen insight. Through the years I've come to rely on the diagnosis as a shorthand way of understanding myself. That I'm any kind of writer at all is almost certainly attributable, at least in part, to my Catholic upbringing and complete inability, from an early age, to feel at home inside the church. Everything I've ever written or even podcasted has on some level been a response to this failure, a lifelong project of self-justification.

•

In the scheme of things, my parents were fairly moderate in their religiosity, Southerners transplanted to the North on account of my father's job, folks for whom churchgoing was a matter of faith and tradition, part of the social order, as normal as brushing one's teeth. When their middle child and only son, at age six, started telling them that he wanted nothing to do with any of it, they did what most parents of their generation and background would have done: they made me go anyway, assuming that over time I would come to appreciate it.

That I never really did was, for a period, a central tension of my childhood, a weekly argument that I couldn't win, one that always ended with me in the back of the car, smushed between my sisters, pouting as we were driven across town to Holy Cross Catholic Church. It wasn't until my teenage years, post-Confirmation, with my resistance reaching new levels of intensity, that my parents began the slow process of surrender, finally acknowledging that my discontent might be more than a passing phase. After the age of sixteen, church became a matter of choice for me. Autonomy, granted. I immediately stopped attending and have rarely been since, save for the odd wedding or funeral. A disappointment to my parents, to be sure, but one that they have managed to accept.

•

As a father, my approach to spiritual matters has in consequence been almost fanatically hands-off, especially so after an early bungled attempt at explaining death to Alice. The conversation happened when she was six and reeling from a trip to the Natural History Museum, where the fate of woolly mammoths, saber-tooth tigers, and ground sloths had been presented in fossilized detail. The experience left her saddled with some heavy questions, and Franny assigned me the task of delivering our response. That night, while tucking Alice in, I made efforts to explain the illusion of death as I understood it, not as a matter of total annihilation but rather as a process of state change. As parental speeches go, it wasn't exactly a ringing success. Alice listened intently and seemed to understand my use of the cloud analogy, how a human life, or any life, was similar to that of a cloud, manifesting for a time when conditions were sufficient, and then taking on new forms as conditions inevitably changed.

But what happens to who you are? she wanted to know. And will we all still see each other afterward?

Crushing. And abundantly clear how the comforting dream of heaven had persisted through the ages. Far easier to explain death as a happy family reunion in Cloud City than as the dissipation of a cloud into acid rain.

But I don't want to lie to her, I said to Franny. The fact is that I don't know.

So why not just tell her that? she said.

I did, I said. Or tried to. I guess I just wanted to add some dimension to it, give her a little something to hold on to. Plus, I really *do* believe in the state change business. First Law of Thermodynamics. I can live with that. I can sleep at night. I feel like it has a foundation.

It's probably fine, Franny said. She's a kid. She'll move on.

And in general, I said, I think we'd be wise to avoid this kind of thing as much as possible until she's older. There's a reason why people's religious identities get solidified in childhood. Your brain is soft. You're impressionable and ripe for indoctrination. Sound judgment is one of the last things to develop in a person, if it ever develops at all. Think of yourself in college. You were a complete fool, right? And so was I. Exercising terrible judgment was *our job*. I didn't really start making any reasonable progress on judgment until I was well into my twenties. I don't think people should be taking on this kind of subject matter until then. I want her to decide for herself.

So do I, said Franny. But she *is* going to need at least a little guidance on the big stuff.

Of course, I said. And we can try our best to give it to her. A nudge here and there along the way. I don't mind if she goes to church with my parents. She can explore.

I *want* her to explore. A little exposure is fine. I just think we should be low-key about it. Nothing dogmatic or heavy-handed. The damage you can do is enormous. Look what just happened when I tried to tell her about state change. She cried for almost an hour.

Franny laughed a little. She's probably gonna be scarred, she said.

She'll never forget this day, I said.

The day her dad told her that she's a rain cloud, Franny said. Doomed to become a mud puddle.

•

To be fair, when I look back on my childhood and the uneasy relationship I had with the church, I have a hard time locating any memories that could truly be characterized as traumatic. No handsy priests, no terrifying Bible camps. Nothing cinematic or ghoulish. My parents, nurturing to an almost ridiculous degree. If I bear any scars, they're of the subtle variety. And I did take from the experience an assortment of positives, too. A basic sense of morality. The Sermon on the Mount. A predisposition to favor the underdog in pretty much any human conflict. And beyond matters of scripture, there was the simple example of my parents' devotional commitment, a form of discipline not entirely dissimilar to that which I've tried, with moderate success, to emulate in my writing life.

Aside from attending a couple of funerals that scared the bejesus out of me, the fact is that my childhood was largely without incident. A blessed little spell of Midwestern suburban boredom, most of which I can't remember. The astonishing fact of how lost it all is. I think, for example, of "my earliest memory," and how over the years I've developed an elaborate narrative around it, telling myself that it was a nightmare involving The Incredible Hulk. I was two, maybe three years old, asleep in my crib, and locked in a terrible trial. The Incredible Hulk was chasing me, the Lou Ferrigno version. I was in a forest. There were witches in a clearing who wanted to cook me in a pot. It was a death dream. But was it *actually* a death dream and did I even know what death was at that age? And do I now? And is this entire story, in the end, just a bunch of confabulated bullshit?

I suppose I feel an obligation to remember when I first learned of my own mortality. If anything in life should stick, you would think it would be something like this. And yet the best I can do, if I'm being truthful, is speculate, sifting through the rubble of my past, piecing together the shards, struggling to build some kind of mosaic.

•

Or maybe it happened in first grade, when there were actual air raid drills. The reality of the end, hitting home. Mrs. Miller, my teacher, walking on crutches, a victim of polio in her youth. And how the instructions were to get down under your desk and cover your head with your hands because this was what you would do if the Soviets ever attacked America in a nuclear war.

•

And for a year and a half I was an altar boy, an unhappy experience for me but my parents were proud. And then one Sunday I fainted during mass, falling backward in my robe, and to this day it's the only time I've ever fainted. And how my mother worried aloud about a brain tumor. And how I wondered if dying was the equivalent of fainting forever, of collapsing backward into nothingness and never waking up. And how I still might believe this right now. *You just faint.*

•

Or the morning I went outside to feed my pet rabbit, Pee-wee, and found him dead on the floor of his cage, frozen solid in the depths of winter. Thinking that he was asleep. Saying: Pee-wee? Shaking the cage again, saying: *Pee-wee?*

•

Or the kid in my neighborhood who cut his finger off by accident. Dismemberment as a preview of disintegration. I was with my buddy Ryan that afternoon, playing in his backyard. The sound of wailing sirens and we ran to follow them, surprised to wind up in front of my house. A teenage boy had been riding his bicycle and the chain had popped off as he was pedaling. He reached down to fix it and his finger got caught in the gear wheel. My dad had been cutting the lawn and heard the scream above the whine of the mower. The boy sliced off the top half of his middle finger and was now in shock in my garage. The paramedics were tending to him. I want to say they put his lost finger in a bag filled with ice. I remember telling kids at school that I saw the bag of ice with the finger in it, but I don't think this was true. I don't think I saw the bag of ice. I don't think I saw the finger.

.

And then in January 1986, when the Space Shuttle *Challenger* exploded. My entire fifth-grade class was in the presentation area at school, watching the launch on a special live feed. The fireball, the smoke, the confusion. And how Mrs. Hopkins, my art teacher, folded forward as if she had been punched in the stomach. And how another teacher crouched down to hug her.

And how a little while later, one of my classmates, a girl named Marianne Jernigan, sidled up next to me and handed me a note. The note was from my very first girlfriend, Julie Werder. I had recently asked her to "go" with me, and she had said yes.

This is for you, Marianne said, whispering.

I opened up the note. The note was from Julie.

The note said: I'M SORRY YOUR DUMPED.

.

In college, out at a bar one night, I told my friend Schuyler, while shooting pool, that the first "big death" of my life was the assassination of John Lennon.

This was bullshit.

The next morning I awoke, hungover, thought back to what I'd said, and felt awful about myself. The truth was that I had no clear memory of Lennon's death, of learning the news, or of even knowing who Lennon was at that age, though probably I did. And yet for some vapid, vaguely bohemian reason I had used the senseless killing of my favorite Beatle as a kind of autobiographical shortcut, in an attempt to explain myself and build my own mythology. A kind of necrophilia.

.

Or maybe, I told myself, it was Ronald Reagan, Lennon's cultural opposite. Just a few weeks later. 1981. My official introduction to mortality. Though of course this wasn't a death—Reagan was only wounded.

I was in a mall with my mother that day, Northridge Mall in Milwaukee. We were in a restaurant, the two of us—or maybe my little sister, Erin, was there. She would have been a toddler then. And my older sister, Lauren. Maybe she was there, too.

And how the room went suddenly silent and I could feel a big shift in its mood. A look of concern falling over my mother's face. Probably I asked her what had happened. Or maybe she didn't tell me but I heard it on the television myself. Or maybe someone at an adjacent table relayed the news and this was how I learned.

Or was it the waiter?

•

In the spring of 1963, my dad was finishing his senior year of high school. His entire childhood had been spent in Morgan City, a small bayou town in south Louisiana. A few weeks before graduation, he was asked to attend a dance in the neighboring town of Plaquemine, about an hour away. One of his classmates, a girl named Louise, had a friend who lived there. The friend had extended an invitation, and Louise asked my dad to be her date and go along for the ride. They drove on what was then a dusty two-lane road, winding through the swampland and cane fields, arriving at the friend's house in early evening, where they joined her family for dinner. My dad had never met any of these people before—about a dozen of them, seated around a long table, one of whom would turn out to be my mother, at the time just a freshman in high school.

This was how my parents first met.

•

Over the years, the story has been told to me on any number of occasions, and with every retelling I get a slightly different version. Certain elements are added, others fall away. My mother had braces and was shy about showing her teeth. My parents didn't really talk beyond a basic introduction. My mom thought my dad was kind of cute. My dad told a joke at the table and nobody laughed but him. My mother's father was stone-faced and thoroughly unimpressed. And on it goes. Hard to say how many of the details are true, but even if they're fictions, they fit the basic profiles of everyone involved.

•

It was just few months later, December of that same

year, a month after JFK was shot, that my Aunt Rosalyn was killed in a horrific car accident just outside Morgan City, on Highway 90, a couple of days before Christmas. The crash took the lives of everybody involved, five people in total. Unholy. My dad, the first in his family to attend college, had just returned home on break, having completed the fall semester at LSU. It was he who answered the door at one in the morning. A couple of highway patrolmen standing on the porch with their hats in their hands.

Rosalyn was only twenty-two, my grandparents' eldest child and their only girl. Her death was a shattering blow. My grandmother—we called her Mimi—had something of a breakdown in the aftermath, her hair turning shock white, much of it falling out. In all the time I knew her, she always wore wigs. My grandfather, Pops, cried easily for the rest of his days, in particular when he said goodbye to family members.

•

Despite the calamity, and at my grandparents' insistence, my father returned to college in January to continue his schooling, hitching a ride with a friend, driving from Morgan City to Baton Rouge, their route taking them through the heart of Plaquemine and directly past my mother's house—only now the house was no longer standing, reduced to a pile of ashes. A fire had destroyed it completely.

Shocked, my dad made his friend stop the car. They pulled into the driveway, amid the charred remains. He climbed out and walked the property, surveying the damage—the unthinkable damage of that season—wondering what might have happened to everyone inside.

Upon arriving back at campus, he went immediately to the library and searched out recent issues of the small-town Plaquemine paper for details. The headlines were easy to find. It had indeed been a house fire. The Christmas tree had gone up just a few days prior, on the first of the year. The parents had been away at a dinner party. The kids were home alone. One of them plugged in the lights. There was a short. Sparks flew. The needles, dry as tinder. The tree going up like a torch. The beautiful old house with a wraparound porch, gutted in a matter of minutes. Fortunately nobody killed.

And this put the matter to rest. Relieved to learn that no lives had been lost, my father, already reeling from his sister's tragic death, returned to his dormitory and fell back into the rhythms of college life as best he could. He would return home every single weekend that semester to tend to his grieving parents, and wouldn't cross paths with my mother again until 1970, in New Orleans, where he was working one of his earliest jobs. They happened to live in the same apartment complex. My mother herself had recently graduated from LSU with a degree in elementary education. They met at a nearby bar. Greetings were exchanged. Dots were connected. A whirlwind, three-month courtship ensued, followed by a sudden engagement. The wedding took place in 1971, in Plaquemine, just a stone's throw from the site of the fire. They've been together ever since.

•

Nearly thirty years to the day after my parents had their fateful first meeting, I graduated high school in suburban Milwaukee. Much as it was for my dad, this period of my life was marked by tragedy. In the fall of my senior year, one of my closest friends, Jimmy McDermott, lost his older brother, Billy, to brain cancer, age 20. My buddies and I, a tight-knit group of six, all bearing witness to Billy in his final days, delirious from chemo, fighting like hell to stay alive. An incredibly vital young man, a former all-state basketball player, snuffed out by a miserable illness before he ever really got the chance to live. The cruelty of his loss scared all of us terribly and put us in something of a nihilistic mood just as we were turning eighteen.

•

The following summer, I went off to college in Boulder, where I grew my hair out and smoked too much pot and became some approximation of a hippie. There was a bright and wonderful energy to it all—reckless and sweet and a little bit dumb—the excitement of reinvention, the vitality of youth in mountain sun. A college experience unfolding according to script, free of any heavy responsibilities, oblivious to darkness, youth behaving as youth should behave. But then in the middle of my junior year, the revelry came to an abrupt end with the suicide death of my close friend, Tom Mallard. The two of us had met in the dorm our freshman year and had just returned home from a semester abroad in Ireland, where on many occasions we had emphatically agreed that we were having the best time of our lives. Not a week after arriving back home in the States, Mallard put a gun to his head in his sister's apartment and pulled the trigger. A colossally shocking and disorienting experience that altered the trajectory of my life.

·

In the weeks immediately following his death, I had difficulty sleeping. There were nightmares, panic attacks, little sobbing fits. I was probably suffering from post-traumatic stress disorder, though I was never officially diagnosed. I never sought mental health treatment, though I almost certainly should have.

There was, too, a fundamental loss of confidence, a deep sense of failure and destabilization. Unable to trust my own eyes. *He had seemed so happy. He had seemed just fine.* The sadness was simply enormous. And all of the terrible guilt. Worried that I had missed something critical. Even more worried that I *hadn't* missed it, but instead had seen it plainly and failed to properly respond.

.

My final three semesters of college were spent in direct reaction to the tragedy. While nominally a film major, I now made the hard turn toward books and began to get serious about my education. Rather than live with friends like a normal twenty-year-old, I instead chose solitude, taking a quiet studio apartment in the back of a house on 10th Street. I quit smoking cigarettes and started hiking on a daily basis, long walks in the mountains, almost always alone. I grew a beard. Read the Beats. All of it, every cliché. There were meditation classes, too, at an ashram in Eldorado Canyon. Driving over in the mornings, parking in the gravel lot. Goats on the property, a couple of Shiba Inus, beautiful views of the Flatirons. With about ten or fifteen other people, all of them significantly older, I would sit on a cushion in a heated Quonset hut while an earthy woman of about sixty, her hair naturally gray and always tied up in braids, led us through the sessions with outrageous serenity. I had no idea what I was doing.

•

From the inside flap of my notebook during this time period, written in heavy bubble letters:

You never get to where you thought you would go and you never go back to where you thought you were.

•

It was also during this time period that I got my first dog on a whim, a border collie, driving through the Rockies with three friends to a cattle ranch in the town of Fruita, not far from the Utah state line. In retrospect I think I wanted a dog because I wanted to prove to myself that I could care for another creature and not have it die tragically due to my lack of proper attention. It had also occurred to me, and not without cause, that being friends with a dog was a hell of a lot safer than being friends with a human being.

The ranch was wide-open and dusty, a rolling expanse of acreage at the desert end of the Rockies. I can still remember the ranchers, a stout young married couple, taking us around back of the house to a chain-link enclosure, where I was handed my puppy, a puff of black and white fur barely larger than my fist. A great thrill. My first fatherhood. After paying the ranchers a hundred bucks, my friends and I left the property and drove out to Moab and went camping for the night. We ate mushrooms in the moonlight and passed the dog around for six hours, trying to decide what I should name him. As we were doing this my friend Patrick kept telling me, over and over again, YOU HAVE A FUCKING DOG, DUDE. THIS DOG IS FUCKING YOURS. It was sometime after 2:00 AM, as we were all peaking, that I named the dog Merlin because, I reasoned, he looked like a wizard. To me, in the darkness, in that state of mind, if you can imagine it, he seemed to be wearing a big white sorcerer's beard.

Hours later, when I sobered up, efforts were made to rescind the decision, but my friends were having none of it. The name stuck. Merlin was with me from that day forward, a constant and ultra-loyal presence all throughout my twenties, a shepherd dog who saw me through the writing of my first novel (which was, of course, all about suicide grief) and who stayed with me right up until I met Franny not long before my thirtieth birthday. We had only been dating for a few months when he fell ill. At first I thought it was only a virus, or that he had simply eaten something funny. I would drop him off at Franny's apartment on my way to work, and she would look after him. Soon enough, though, he stopped eating entirely, and his condition visibly worsened. We took him in to the vet for a scan and were informed that he had cancer. Hemangiosarcoma. It was terminal. A massive tumor on his spleen. I wept. Franny wept, too. It was the first time I ever told her that I loved her.

WE DIDN'T HAVE a traditional wedding. Franny's parents were getting up in age and already were in failing health by then, dealing with various ailments, buried in a rising pile of medical bills. Paying for any kind of ceremony would've been a stretch. And aside from that, Franny had zero interest in the classical trappings of bridehood. To be the center of attention for any reason had always been anathema to her. The thought of having to wear a princess gown before an audience in an emotionally loaded moment was, for a woman of her Nordic temperament, an absolutely mortifying possibility. Not to mention the fact that her mother might show up at the reception with a box of orthodontia, or one of her old training bras.

·

For a short while, the possibility of New Orleans was considered, some kind of springtime celebration in the land of my family roots, but after pricing it out, engaging with the tedium of table settings and flower arrangements, we quickly decided to scrap the idea, opting instead for a trip to Europe, just the two of us, and a ten-minute ceremony at Town Hall in Positano, Italy. The wedding and the honeymoon, all rolled into one. Technically, it wasn't an elopement—there was nothing secret about it. And the logistics were surprisingly uncomplicated. A short bit of paperwork at the consulate in Los Angeles prior to departure, and off we went. While our parents were disappointed to miss the official proceedings, it was agreed that we would, upon our return, host a party among close family and friends to raise a glass and mark the occasion.

.

What I remember most about the ceremony itself is the fact that neither Franny nor I had thought to prepare any kind of formal vows. The mayor of Positano, who officiated, rambled through her protocol in rapid Italian, hardly a word of which we understood, and then, following the exchange of rings, we were invited to share some thoughts of our own. All we could do was burst into laughter, explaining a bit sheepishly that we had nothing on hand. With the mayor's encouragement, we both took turns improvising, standing there on the patio, with its breathtaking views, each of us talking about how we would love the other for the rest of our lives. And as we were making these remarks, big gusts of wind began to kick up, howling in from the Gulf of Salerno. Franny, holding on to her hairdo. The mayor, with her big toothy smile, struggling to keep the pages of her script in order. I immediately fell into magical thinking, telling myself that it was some kind of omen, a good one, possibly our grandparents and other interested parties, sending good wishes from the great beyond.

.

All these years later, though, and taking into account everything we've endured since then—the five lost pregnancies and the heartbreak over Oscar in particular—I can't help but look back and translate the moment in a different register. A picture-perfect evening in one of the most beautiful places on earth, an absolute fairytale tableau, nothing but good fortune on our minds—and then the big winds blowing in, seemingly from out of nowhere, whipping against our faces as we extemporized our vows, a not-so-subtle reminder that any future, no matter how beautifully imagined, is always fundamentally insecure.

THE THIRD MISCARRIAGE was the worst of the five. The baby was conceived in the beginning of spring and held on into summer. At six weeks we had seen a heartbeat, which made it feel real and exciting, as statistics were now squarely in our favor, but at ten weeks all was lost. I got the news while en route to a meeting. Franny was on the other end of the line, sobbing in stirrups at the doctor's office. She had gone in alone. It had been decided that, having seen the heartbeat, it was okay for her to go by herself. A move rooted in superstition, a gesture of confidence. We wanted to behave as if everything was going to turn out fine.

The baby didn't measure, she told me, barely able to speak. There isn't any heartbeat. I thought there would be a heartbeat. I wanted to send you a video of the baby's heartbeat.

She dissolved into sobs. Pure misery. We remained on the phone for another fifteen minutes, the conversation unfolding in small, sad circles, and then, when it was finished, I got out of my car and walked into my meeting looking like I'd just seen a ghost.

.

The following morning Franny was scheduled to return to the doctor's office to have a D&C so that the fetus could be extracted and sent off to a lab for testing, but overnight she started miscarrying naturally. We awoke at dawn to bloody sheets.

I intercepted Alice, then age three, just as she entered the room, ushering her into the kitchen, feeding her breakfast, getting her ready for preschool, while Franny went into the bathroom and bore the brunt of it. The fetus, our child, gender undetermined, came out of her body and fell into the toilet and sank to the bottom of the bowl. Thinking we would need him/her for testing, she fished him/her out of the water with a large kitchen spoon and put him/her inside of a Tupperware container, all kitchen items provided by me at Franny's request, both of which were handed to her while she wept in mostly silent spasms, arm extended from a crack in the door, as Alice stood by, asking me what was happening and if Mommy was feeling sick.

Flustered, I coaxed her back out to the television and sat her on the couch and put on some cartoons. I then returned to the bathroom, opened the door, and went inside. The floor was covered in wide smears of blood. Franny was on her knees by the toilet. Her crying was primal. I crouched down to hug her and she sobbed into my shoulder and there was a feverish heat coming off of her body as she shook. I kissed her on the cheek and caught one of her teardrops in my mouth and, tasting its saltiness, told her how sorry I was.

.

Two hours later, in the doctor's office, Franny informed the nurse that our latest lost fetus was stored inside of a Tupperware container in her handbag on the floor.

So that testing can be done, she explained.

The doctor then stepped into the room, as if on cue, and, having caught the conversation midstream, informed us, with pity in his eyes, that the sample was now contaminated, and by "sample" he meant "your child," and we nodded and shook our heads and felt instantly silly and confessed that we should have understood the contamination factor, but failed to on account of the chaos, and by "chaos" we meant "the loss of our child."

.

After the consultation was over and it was just the two of us in the room, Franny asked me what we should do with the Tupperware container and, wanting desperately to be helpful in a way that felt concrete, I told her that I would take care of it here at the doctor's office so that we wouldn't have to do it at home, the prospect of which seemed, at first blush, unbearable, as I imagined it would involve dropping the container into the foul-smelling dumpster in the alley out back.

Stepping into the hallway, I approached the first nurse that I saw. After explaining to her, briefly, what had happened, I asked her, quietly, to please dispose of the Tupperware, and by "Tupperware" I meant "my child," and she said yes, yes, of course she would, no problem. And so I handed this woman, a complete stranger, the remains of my third lost child, stored inside of a container made of petroleum, and moments after the exchange she presumably threw him/her into the trash and continued on with her workday.

It's something that I'll always regret, though I suppose I should forgive myself for it, considering how discombobulated I was that day. The fact that it didn't occur to me to bury the fetus, or otherwise offer a more dignified send-off, feels like an outrageous error in judgment. But this was what I did. I handed the Tupperware to the nurse, then walked back down the hall to get Franny, and together we left the office, heads down, moving through the crowded waiting room, filled to bursting with an assortment of pregnant women in various stages of happy rotundity. After taking the elevator down to the garage, we climbed into the car and pulled out into traffic, headed home, defeated, the sun beating down on everything, entirely too bright. The stereo playing bad pop music at low volume. I turned it off.

This is bullshit, Franny said, very quietly.

I know, I said.

I'm just sick of it, she said.

I know, I said, and offered her my hand. She squeezed it.

I'm pissed, she said.

I know.

It just sucks.

I know.

I'm so *pissed*.

It's out of our control, I heard myself say, a little bit too loudly. It's just nature doing what nature does, and nature always knows what it's doing.

I regretted the words almost as soon as they left my mouth.

Franny began to cry in her soft, quiet way.

I have no idea what I'm doing, I said.

·

It's like gambling, I texted my friend Timmy later that

day, in an attempt at explanation.

> *your wife gets pregnant, and you feel*
> *this dual thrill: victory & danger*
> *the stakes have been raised*
> *your experience of life is elevated*
> *you've rolled a 7*
> *or, like, a series of 7s*
> *and as the pregnancy progresses*
> *the chips are stacking up*
> *and people are cheering*
> *and then all at once your luck runs out*
> *and you roll a snake eyes*
> *and the air goes out of the room*
> *and everyone groans*
> *and the dealer mops up your winnings*
> *coldly & without remorse*

·

That night in bed, Franny and I lay there like a couple of zombies, unable to sleep. We watched television until well after midnight, several old episodes of *Saturday Night Live*, hoping to go numb, then turned it off and adjusted to the darkness, trying to drift. But no luck. A certain restlessness was still working on both of us, our minds still churning, the wounds of the day still fresh.

Busy brain, Franny said, pressing up against me,

resting her chin on my shoulder.

You need anything? I said.

Propofol, she said.

I could read, I said. But I'd need to turn on the light. I feel like if I read something, I might fall asleep. But I know you can't sleep with the light on.

You can't turn on the light, she said. But you can tell me a story.

A story, I said.

Make something up, she said.

Like, a bedtime story?

Or just tell me one of your favorites.

I thought for a moment and then told her about a story I used to teach back when I was in graduate school, a story by Lydia Davis.

I can't remember the name of it, I said. It's, like, a line or two long. Incredibly short but also somehow perfect. And it's all about thinking, and how if you're thinking too much and you want to stop yourself from thinking, all you have to do is keep your eyeballs still. And the best part about it, I said, is that it's actually true, and if you actually do that—if you actually keep your eyeballs still—then your thinking will actually stop.

So you're telling me to keep my eyeballs still? she said.

Try it, I said.

I CAN REMEMBER the exact moment when I knew that I wanted to marry her. We were at dinner, one of our earliest dates, a little Italian restaurant in Venice Beach. Her hair was damp. She had just arrived. I went to stand as she sat down. Her cheeks were flushed. I forget exactly what was said. I only remember her smiling, and that she was wearing her black jacket, and that she was looking at me. And I remember knowing in that instant, as she looked at me and smiled, that I loved her. Nothing dramatic about it. Just a small, quiet jolt somewhere in the recesses of my being. But at the same time unmistakable. I knew. And this feeling of knowing was something akin to relief.

•

But is this true? I can't help but wonder. Did I *really*

know? Did this moment *actually* happen in the way that I recall? Some version of it certainly did, but it's possible and even likely that over time I've come to embellish it as a way of apprehending the past, giving our history some definition and a sweet cinematic beginning. Because this is what humans do. We tell ourselves nice little stories and believe them as if they were true. But they aren't actually true. At best, they're only kind of true. And the more that a person remembers a thing, scientists say, the less likely it is to be accurate. With each retelling, the essence gets lost. Which, if true, leaves me wrestling with a fairly big conundrum: If my sense of self is constructed from memories, but the memories are not to be trusted, then how am I supposed to have any kind of clear sense of self?

I'm never entirely who I think I am.

Also: what the fuck actually happened?

And how has all of this time gone by?

·

Here we are, nearly fifteen years removed from those big gusts of wind on that patio in Positano. And of course it went by in a blink. In some ways, we've gotten more than we bargained for; in other ways we've gotten less. That's life. That's love. All of it is trauma, in the end. Marriage is hard and it's divine. It

136

can be so effortless. It can take so much work. In my better moments, I experience it as a kind of practice. Over the years I've found that it's less about a happy magical union among disparate souls than it is about fracturing. Nobody ever told me this. How marriage breaks you open in a thousand different places, forcing you to reveal yourself and to confront your own depths and, if you're lucky, to see your own shortcomings for exactly what they are. A kind of holy ordeal, a test of endurance, complete with daily rituals of love and forgiveness. The little things. The golden moments. A hand placed inside of another hand. The kiss before bed. The code words. The apologies. The fucking.

And how accumulated grief can have an impact on all of it. The miscarriages. Oscar. Alice having a panic attack about Cesar Chavez dying in his sleep. Franny and I, dealing with everything as it comes, trying our best, bearing the sacred weight of our shared wounds, most of the time in silence.

The two of us in bed, not even 7:00 AM, racing to have sex before the kids wake up—and the grief is there. Something else nobody ever told me. How even the act of fucking becomes freighted with unexpected meanings and associations when you're heartbroken over a child. To have to face one another like that in the wake of it all, bodies slapping together, faces just inches apart, doing the very thing that brought you all of this heartbreak in the first place. And yet there we go, doing it anyway. Trying. And sometimes it can all be too much. The emotion can overtake us. The guilt. Things can get stirred up. We'll lie there after the fact, feeling agitated, rather than properly spent. But other days, on better mornings, when our minds will leave us alone, it functions exactly as it's supposed to, as a temporary reprieve and an act of vengeance against all that has befallen us, and will eventually befall us down the line.

•

And probably it's true, according to conventional wisdom, that we should be in greater communication about all of our feelings on a daily basis. Pop psychology would almost certainly advocate for this sort of thing. I can't say that we're doing it all perfectly, but I do believe that we're doing alright, even if we seem to have arrived at a more judicious approach to language when it comes to our deepest pains. In my experience, there's only so much benefit to be derived from keeping a running tab on the sadness—a sadness that will, I suspect, come and go in waves for the rest of our lives. We'll always be sad about Oscar's disability—of course we will. It would break the heart of any decent parent. But to talk about it too much is, I think, to make a profound error in emphasis, and would do a disservice to ourselves, and to both of our kids, these people who have brought infinitely more joy to our lives than they could ever do otherwise. So yes, of course, the sadness is there, monolithic, immoveable, deserving of some recognition. And it will to continue to be there, existing right alongside the joy for as long we live. But to document its presence in meticulous fashion would be like talking about the ocean all the time, running color commentary as the waves roll in, one after the other. You could no sooner do away with child-related grief than you could do away with the waves. So what's there to talk about, really? *The rocks, the sand, the water.* It's always the same. Just take a deep breath, call it out silently by name, and get on with it.

And for the most part, this is what we try to do. It's all we *can* do, really, in the blur of domesticity, with its deadlines and school commutes and medical appointments all over town. At times, I can feel a sense of enormous pride over the simple fact that we're managing. The triumph of survival. It isn't easy. Franny in particular has endured so much. Five lost pregnancies and a disabled child would send most mothers over the edge. And on top of it all, she had to cope with the illness and death of both of her parents, absorbing these heavy losses in rapid succession, and doing so with an uncommon amount of grace. It can be hard not to marvel at her strength, her ability to compartmentalize. And it can be equally hard not to fret over her tendency to bury her feelings so well. But what exactly is she supposed to do? Fall to the floor in her grief? There's no time for that. And there are no rules here. Everyone handles this shit differently. We're both adult humans in our forties, parents in the thick of the process. Suffering was always promised to us, and here it is. Death is promised to us, too. If we ever had any illusions on this front, they were dispensed with long ago.

The truth is that I've never loved Franny more purely than I have in our lowest moments, when I've witnessed her in a doctor's office, getting obliterated by difficult news, and then, just hours later, watching as she sets up for Alice's birthday party with a smile on her face. Always bearing the unbearable, bending under the weight of it but never fully breaking. Always, for the most part, in control—certainly more so than I ever am. My stoic, patient Swede. And me, the Franco-Sicilian motor-mouth, far less patient, my entire life and career dedicated to mapping my insides. The two of us locked in a shared destiny, working across our respective solitudes in a state of mutual incomprehension. The sheer oddity of an intimate relationship. To live with the impossibility of ever fully knowing the other—but trying anyway. And how absurd it can all be, muddling through the inherent confusions. The miscommunications. The white lies we tell. The merciful little omissions. The losses of temper and the reconciliations. The incredible jumble of feelings that we have for one another on any given day, many of which are in direct conflict. And yet beneath all of the surface tumult, there remains the great calm, the sense of ease, the trust, the deep familiarity, the love. The fact that we still like the same movies and laugh at all the same jokes. That we evoke in one another lost feelings from our similar childhoods in the Upper Midwest. Together we move through the days, locked in this strange performance. A kind of beautiful, awkward dance. Two imperfect people making an imperfect life together. All of it built on a single, improvised promise made during a windstorm in Italy.

OSCAR WAS ABOUT six months old when Franny first noticed the fist—how he would clench his little left hand when she picked him up, the arm fixed behind his back as if he were expecting to be cuffed. There was also the issue of his attention, and how on occasion he would seem to drift off, eyes open, staring out into space, unresponsive to voices or attempts at physical communication. The episodes never lasted long, a few seconds at most, but were noticeable enough to cause some concern. *Is he having petit mal seizures?* we couldn't help but wonder. Even a cursory glance at the internet could send both of us into quiet frenzies of panic. Franny in particular was fragile around such topics. She had been struggling for months with postpartum depression, just as she had with Alice. With both of our kids, I handled the bulk of the childcare duties in the first year, night duty in particular, as

Franny's blues tended to come on most strongly after dark. Doctor's appointments were also dicey. I did most all of those.

It was at Oscar's six-month appointment that I mentioned the fist and the possible seizures to Dr. Weintraub, our pediatrician. I can still see the furrow in her brow as she looked down at him on the examination table, noodling with his arm, playing with his hand a bit, frowning slightly, suggesting that I have it checked by a pediatric neurologist as a precautionary measure. Pulling out her notepad, she scribbled down her chicken scratch referral, and moments later I was standing on the sidewalk on Wilshire on a breezy and unseasonably warm day in January, cars whizzing by, a police helicopter buzzing overhead. Outwardly I was calm, but at chest level there was an acute sense of dread. I remember looking down at Oscar in his stroller and actually saying aloud to him, very quietly: *I think you're going to be the one that I have to worry about.*

.

The ten days that followed are a period of time that I'm capable of recalling with a sense of nostalgia—the final ten days of our "typical life," when we were all still removed from more harrowing realities. Part of me, I think, deep down, understood even then that we were in for a difficult road. And Franny was aware of it, too. We knew. We didn't really speak of it, though, each of us holding our fears close to the vest, as if discussing any hard possibilities might somehow cause them to manifest. And apart from that, there was the simple matter of reflexive denial, the wanting to remain unaware. Never underestimate a parent's ability to achieve this feat in a situation of this nature. Even a person like me, who likes to think of himself as sober-minded and open to hard truths, had zero ability, at this stage, to seriously engage with an idea as heartrending as cerebral palsy. The fact is that it wasn't in my field of possibility. If something was wrong, I told myself, then surely it was fixable. And besides, nothing official had been communicated yet. Everything at this point was precautionary, speculative. We were simply following Weintraub's advice in the interest of ruling things out. To get too wound up about anything beyond that was out of order and premature. Together, Franny and I made a solemn vow that we would refrain from any neurotic Googling, and both of us, against the odds, managed to obey the moratorium for the ensuing ten days.

.

The pediatric neurologist at Cedars was a tall, reed-thin,

bespectacled man named Richard Zabitsky—a brilliant doctor, according to Weintraub, but one with the bedside manner of a large fence post. While giving Oscar a thorough physical examination, he suggested to me, with unnerving neutrality, that my son may have suffered a stroke in utero. But without a clear picture of his brain, he added, it would be impossible to make any kind of true diagnosis. As such, it was his recommendation that Oscar undergo a brain MRI as soon as possible, a procedure that would involve a brief period of anesthesia. I was instructed to call a certain number to coordinate scheduling at the hospital's imaging center. The procedure, Zabitsky assured me, was safe and straightforward and would last about an hour. I thanked him and went home.

It was three weeks later, after the MRI had been conducted, after I had watched Oscar be anesthetized, his little body laid out flat at the mouth of the machine, that my phone rang at around midday on a sunny Thursday in February. Whenever I think back and try to pinpoint the exact moment when I knew for certain that my life had changed, I tend to return to this call, and the receptionist from Cedars on the line, and me in our old house on 4th Street, the worn-out Spanish bungalow with the citrus trees out back.

We need to get you in for an appointment, the receptionist said. The doctor would like to go over some results.

I asked her what was happening. My heart racing suddenly, a sick feeling. She told me that I needed to come in for the appointment and the doctor would go over everything then.

Why don't you tell me right now? I said.

She wouldn't tell me.

I think you should tell me now, I said.

She wouldn't tell me.

I lost my shit.

I remember, I think I can remember, being in my bedroom, standing by the screen door that opened out to the deck. It was always too dark in that room, but the lawn outside was bright. I seem to recall dropping into a crouch, barking into the receiver, demanding that this woman tell me what the *fuck* was going on with my son. But of course she wouldn't tell me. Hospital policy. *This isn't something we can do over the phone, sir.* My face flushed red with anger, a surge of terrible fear in my chest. A tangerine tree outside, bearing fruit. Possibly a hummingbird.

This, I like to tell myself, was when everything suddenly shifted, when the creeping dread that had been plaguing me for weeks finally brought me to the point of overwhelm, just as the diagnostic process reached its miserable crescendo. I have also sometimes told myself over the years that this was the precise moment when my excessively long childhood reached its conclusion, the brief hard flash in time when at long last I finished growing up and instead just started aging.

•

A couple of hours later, I was en route to Cedars to receive official word on Oscar's condition, driving silently down 3rd Street in the Jeep, no radio, nothing, pulling into the lot outside the Steven Spielberg Building, trying my best to focus on my breathing. Oscar, meanwhile, was sweetly oblivious in back, buckled into his car seat, babbling at the passing cars as we drove. I found a spot not far from the entrance, killed the ignition, and climbed out of my seat slowly, a distinct heaviness in my limbs. Strapping on the BabyBjörn, I cinched the belt around my waist and carried my son inside against my chest.

I don't really remember much about entering the building or taking the elevator upstairs or checking in at the desk or making any small talk with the receptionist, who was probably in no mood to receive me after the way that I had treated her on the phone. All that I remember clearly is being in a fluorescently-lit examination room, where I sat on a low stool with Oscar for a couple of minutes, bouncing him nervously on my knee, before the door swung open and a group of three doctors entered the room, led by Zabitsky, a little pack of them, moving in ominous formation. There was an older doctor to Zabitsky's right, a distinguished-looking gentleman with a helmet of silver hair, and to the left stood a young, female doctor, not a day older than thirty, with a pixie cut and horn-rimmed glasses. I have a hard time recalling their specific facial features— even Zabitsky is now a blur to me—but I'll never forget how noticeably sad they all seemed, the young woman in particular, who appeared as though she might start crying. More than any particular image or sound, it is the energy of these moments that has stayed with me most vividly through the years, the room seeming to vibrate with a heightened level of gravity, as if all of us might fall through the floor at any moment. And how, as Zabitsky began to explain to me, in his dry, robotic patter, all that Oscar's diagnosis entailed or could possibly entail—*hemiplegia, right hemisphere, left-side paralysis*—I interrupted him suddenly and blurted out, of all things, *I just want him to be able to go to Harvard.*

You never quite know what you'll say in a moment like this until it happens. A doctor stands before you and tells you in no uncertain terms that your dreams for your child, your only son, have been altered forever. The words leave the doctor's mouth, travel through the air, hit your ears. And you say something. You feel obligated to say something. How could you *not* say something?

And yet at the same time it is absurd to think that I, or anyone, could be expected to muster any kind of cogent response to information of this nature. My son's future, completely undone in a single instant. Not a fatal diagnosis, no. And thank god. But a diagnosis that was, in its way, fatal to the future—my imagined version of it, anyway—the hopeful dream of a friendly future, a future that had Oscar experiencing the lucky accident of a carefree childhood, a childhood more or less like my own, one without a litany of therapy appointments, the necessity of daily medications, the use of adaptive equipment. A childhood free of excessive feelings of alienation, of difficult otherness or ostracization. A childhood free, for the most part, of the merciless cruelty and deep insensitivities of other human beings. The dream of him playing soccer, running fast on a wide green field, experiencing the thrill of scoring a goal. The dream of hiking Mt. Kilimanjaro together in his teenage years. The simple, normal dream that he would experience the joyous energy of youth absent any major health concerns. All of these dreams, in that moment, in that little doctor's office, under those dismal fluorescent lights, were either totally obliterated or called into question. And when it happened, when the news entered my ears and registered in my brain, the best I could think to say was something about Harvard, something only marginally related to any kind of dream that I'd ever consciously had about my son's future. The truth is that I don't give a fuck about Harvard. But on that day, in that moment, I did.

Zabitsky, I recall—a Harvard man himself— lowered his gaze in response to my response, telling me in a soft and even more robotic voice that the diagnosis was often associated with epilepsy, and might also involve cognitive delays.

I can't recall how, if at all, I responded to this news. If I said something intelligible, it is now lost to me. Here again, though, I do recall the physical sensation of the moment. It was as though I had been kicked in the sternum by a large horse. My breath leaving me. The clear and unmistakable sensation that something inside of me was breaking and breaking permanently, and I could feel it break as it broke.

•

How much longer the appointment lasted after that is anyone's guess. Probably fifteen minutes or so. I have no idea. It doesn't really matter. There was, for a short while, the going over of next steps, some discussion of basic treatment protocols and what we could expect. The silver-haired doctor explaining the likely necessity of physical, occupational, and speech therapies. The handing over of a couple of brochures and business cards as he and Zabitsky wished me well, each of them shaking my hand firmly before exiting the room, leaving me alone with the young female doctor—a counselor, she explained. Her job was to help parents like me adjust to the complicated demands of their new realities. Did I have any questions or need any immediate referrals, she wanted to know. I told her I did not. She then spent a minute or so cooing at Oscar, telling me how adorable he was, and how sorry she was for all that we were going through. I thanked her. She handed me her card and told me that she would be available to Franny and me in the weeks ahead should we need any assistance on anything whatsoever. I thanked her again, and she walked me to the door.

•

On the way home, I called my parents and shared the difficult news. I was upset but controlled, reeling but relatively calm. In shock. They, in turn, were upset but controlled, also presumably in shock. The idea was to lower the boom on them first, and to use this as a dry run for having to go home and explain it all to Franny, who had been texting me incessantly throughout the appointment, waiting for word. Even now, with the doctor's verdict fresh in my mind, there was still some level of denial at work—not just for me, but for my parents as well. A natural response, I suppose, to a heartbreak of this magnitude. The wild grasping for hope, all three of us desperate to believe that it might all turn out fine somehow. My father imploring me to stay positive. My mother talking about how she wouldn't stop praying, how she believed in her heart that he would end up okay. All of us commiserating about rapid medical advancements, the mapping of the genome, and how, with today's digital technology, anything on earth seemed possible.

It was in the middle of all this chatter that I pulled up outside of our house, parking on the street under our jacaranda tree. Glancing to my right, I was startled to see Franny standing alone on the front walkway, midway to the curb, arms folded tightly across her chest. She had been waiting at the window, watching, on edge. With my parents talking into my ear, I rolled down my window, looked at her with a pained expression, gave a tiny shrug, and felt my head turn side-to-side. That was all it took. She mouthed the words "oh no"—I could make them out easily from that distance—a far more intelligent response than my knee-jerk Harvard nonsense from earlier. *Oh no*, I could see her saying. *Oh no. Oh no. Oh no.*

WHAT I'M LEFT with, I wrote in my notebook, *is a knot of suffering in my chest—but it's important to note that the knot has always been there. Nothing new. Nothing special about it. Human condition. Entirely standard. And maybe now my knot is a little bit bigger than most (?), and for the rest of my life I'll be working to untangle it, trying to make it smaller and more manageable. And probably this is the point of my (or any?) existence: to untangle one's knot in painstaking fashion and make with the thread some kind of meaning?*

And then over to the left, in the margin:

We are the accumulation of negative space.

•

The central challenge, I find—one of the central challenges—is that there's really no way to be consistently, predictably elegant when responding to suffering that is centered on a child. I wish I knew how to do it. I don't. When a person is wounded by this kind of grief, the wound is never clean. No easy repairs, no straight-line scar where the sutures used to be. No time limits, either. And certainly no closure. You don't just move on from a thing like this. You move forward with it. Again the mantra: It's like learning to carry fire.

Tough shit.

·

A game I'll sometimes play, on certain days, in certain moods, is to remind myself of world historical figures who had it way worse than I do, who endured unthinkable miseries but found a way to triumph in spite of it all. Nelson Mandela and his twenty-seven years of unjust imprisonment. Anne Frank in the attic with her diary. Helen Keller finding her way out of the darkness. People who have absorbed some of the most dreadful absurdities that life can serve up, but who somehow managed to retain their grace and keep a firm hold on the best of themselves.

And as I'm thinking of such people I might be sitting in, say, a coffee shop, trying to get some work done, and in the midst of this process my thoughts might suddenly darken, and I'll find myself, for example, cataloging the other patrons in the shop—the predictable Hollywood dipshits in their designer tennis shoes and vintage T-shirts, with their eight-dollar lattes and their Very Important Projects. And the fancy housewives with their stupid fancy dogs, bioengineered for Instagram. And the annoying couple with the endless tattoos and the matching nose rings who seem to be posing at all times, having reduced their entire grating lives down to a guerrilla marketing campaign. And in the span of just a few seconds, I will have gone from a high-minded attempt at reframing to a vicious cavalcade of petty insults, from pondering Gandhi and his courageous Salt March to silently castigating the businessman to my left, in his stupid blue button-down, loud-talking into his phone with his sunglasses resting on his shiny pink head, the self-important corporate motherfucker.

And the reason for this dramatic shift in mood, for this sudden hard turn from light to dark, is the fact that I've just laid eyes on a mother and her little boy, a boy about the same age as Oscar, a typical little kid, and he's running or playing or walking or simply holding a sippy cup without any difficulty, and the mere sight of this child and his able little body will cause the knot in my chest to instantly double in size, the mess of its tangle made anew, and when this happens a cloud of gloom will descend, with its flashes of rage and its thundering sadness, and after going through all my dismal color commentary, I might find myself gathering my things in a hurry, jamming my laptop into my bag, telling myself that I'm better off working at home in the garage, away from all these people, because the happiest of all lives is a busy solitude, and then I'll be out the door.

·

Twice on the podcast over the past decade I've talked with the poet Matthew Zapruder, most recently when he was touring in support of his collection entitled *Father's Day*, which, among other things, deals with the gross implosions of American public life and his experiences as the father of a child on the autism spectrum. For us, there was an immediate and natural bond, a couple of middle-aged dads trying our best to navigate difficult waters and adjust to unexpected realities.

At the end of *Father's Day*, Zapruder includes a short afterword called "Late Humanism" in which he assesses his own collection and reflects on his writing about his son. "My son of course is not a symbol," he says—

> . . . *nor, for that matter, a diagnosis. In these poems, it is not he but my image of him, animated by my hope and terror and love, that becomes a symbol. I hope that is okay with him,*

and that whenever he is old enough to read this, he will understand why it was impossible for me to be a poet and write the truth without including those feelings. I hope he will know that I realize my fear was my own problem. It was something for me to get through so I could see what has always been possible. I can also see now that the hope and understanding I feel more each day were already revealing themselves in the poems. I just needed to catch up.

I admire this essay, which delivered a hit of inspiration and helped bring some clarity to the muddiness of my own thinking. I said as much to Zapruder when he was here, explaining how this passage in particular had offered some critical insight into how I might approach the writing of my book.

It can be difficult, I told him, trying to strike the right balance. What to put in, what to leave out. The concern over misrepresenting something, or doing unnecessary damage, or saying something miserably dumb. The desire to be both accurate and open but at the same time not weirdly exploitative or despairing to a withering degree. I know that I need to address the darkness, for example, but I don't want to get to the point where I'm bludgeoning anyone with it, if that makes sense.

Zapruder, listening carefully, remained silent for

a beat, then shared a story about fellow poet Robert Hass, explaining how Hass, whenever he got stuck on a poem, would often address the issue by "putting the problem in the poem."

Which is to say, Zapruder said, if you're struggling with something, uncomfortable in some way, then maybe the best approach is simply to talk about *that* in the book. Chekhov said as much, too. Address it directly—aware of the fact that it's not about solving anything on the page. Just to state the problem clearly, on its own, can be enough.

·

In that case, I might talk about the feelings of deep inadequacy that can still rise up from time to time. The enormous guilt that will probably always live somewhere in the pit of me, occasionally malignant, other times in remission. The weariness that can overtake me when I feel like I'm performing resilience and "okay-ness" in the company of friends and family in an effort to be socially acceptable. The confusion I can still feel over the errors that I've made and the degree to which I'm responsible for them. How to make sense of it all. Process it. Put it into some kind of perspective.

·

Forgiveness, I suppose, would be the fundamental issue at hand. Or one of the fundamental issues. There seem to be multiple fundamental issues. Multiple problems. Which itself is a problem.

The problems.

.

Or maybe there are no problems. Maybe the problems are phantoms. Maybe what I perceive as problems are simply mental narratives that I've constructed which together deliver my false sense of self, and what I actually need to do is wake up from my sentient sleepwalk and relinquish my grievances and exist in a state of exalted liberation and deep acceptance. But so far I haven't been able to muster that, which can also sort of feel like a problem.

.

It is a problem trying to write about the crushing sadness and capture it accurately, without hyperbole, and with some jokes thrown in to make the process bearable. It is a problem trying to balance all of the pathos with the many genuine moments of happiness and normality that can exist on a given day. It is a problem trying to decide how and whether to address the very worst of the grief, the grief in its most agonizing and intimate forms—what it feels like, for example, to lie awake with Franny on the rare nights when she loses her composure and tells me how terribly guilty she feels, how afraid for our children's futures. And how as I lie there in silence, witnessing this, I can feel like I'm slowly disintegrating.

Is it necessary to go here? I can wonder. *Is it appropriate? Is it helpful?*

•

And then there's the problem of how and whether to talk about the fact that I can sometimes spend entire afternoons, even now, so monumentally heartsick about Oscar that I can hardly say a word. Or how to admit, in writing, that I feel like I failed my wife as we moved through our miscarriages. How I worry that I didn't understand the medical landscape clearly enough and didn't make enough of the right decisions at that point in the process. Honest mistakes, I tell myself, but mistakes all the same, mistakes that came with a cost and brought pain to my entire family. And how at times I can feel so awful about it all, so wrecked by the miserable ache of it, that I can fall into my Wile E. Coyote mode, imagining myself strapped to a rocket at the rim of the Grand Canyon, striking a match and lighting the wick. Is it necessary or even the least bit useful to go into all of this excruciating tediousness? I don't know.

•

And this doesn't even begin to take into account the issues of basic biology and the fog surrounding the pregnancy, and how we still don't fully understand exactly how all of it happened, and likely we never will. And how the obstetrician assured us that the emergency C-section and the umbilical cord and Oscar's placement in the birth canal were definitely not to blame—though we can't help but wonder if this was all simply a ploy to avoid a medical malpractice suit. And how other doctors have, in the intervening years, cast some doubt on this assessment, while others still have explained that it was likely some unlucky combination of both, a traumatic birth coupled with unlucky genetics. But if this is the case and the neurological issues presented, even partially, in utero, we then have to contend with the maddening fact that they were somehow missed on all the ultrasounds. And how did that happen? And what would we have done had we caught them? And what a spectacular mindfuck that can be. And so on.

•

There comes a point, I think, at which the problems themselves become, in the aggregate, a new kind of problem, in the sense that it's almost impossible to

163

unpack them in any kind of constructive manner. The more you look at them, the more they seem to multiply and blend and fold in on themselves. It all has a way of becoming unbearably dense in a hurry, a black hole of sadness and confusion, drawing you into its depths.

.

Or maybe, I sometimes think, it's really just a matter of psychological control. Maybe what I'm doing here is catastrophizing—or maybe not. Maybe these issues are genuinely, objectively large and emotionally vexing to an extreme degree. And when the details of a tragedy surpass a certain scale and depth of impact, they begin to defy language. And when something defies language, it defies thought. You can find yourself utterly confounded in the face of it all, feeling as if somebody just hit you over the head with a cinderblock and then asked you to share your deepest secrets.

.

Emotions, I find, have a way of becoming bearable over time. The feelings, however leveling, are always temporary. But to speak of the darkest aspects of one's trauma, to dig down deep and try to get real about it, to bring oneself into direct contact with its heavy and immovable nature, and to then arrive at something resembling insight? All I can tell you is that it's a problem. And where it leaves me, and where it leaves Franny, and where it seems to leave most anyone who engages with it in a serious way, is in a small, private place of quiet surrender. Which is what, I think, these kinds of tragedies have a tendency to do: they beat you and they beat you and they beat you, and then they put you in a little mental cul-de-sac where words are essentially useless and the powers of logic reach their terminus, and the only thing you can really do is try your best to let go of it all, to relinquish the past and accept what is, and get on with the rest of your life.

THREE OR FOUR times a year, I'll have dinner and drinks with my old friend, Mikhail Moralis, over in Silver Lake. That or we'll catch a game at Dodger Stadium, sitting in the cheap seats, eating peanuts, drinking beer. Moralis is the biggest and most knowledgeable baseball fan I've ever met. He also knows more about film history and rock music than anyone I know. A kind of cultural polymath, a barrel-chested man of unusually large appetites, six-foot-three, with a deep, raspy voice, born and raised on an organic farm in Petaluma, the child of activist hippies and a lifelong San Francisco Giants fan.

Among my friends, Mikhail is notable for having made a consistent effort through the years to check in on Oscar, always careful to ask about Alice as well, leaning into the situation rather than shying away. A real mensch. We met in graduate school nearly two decades ago, in Cubby Selby's workshop, and have remained close friends ever since. A bit of an odd pairing. Moralis, the bohemian free spirit, a poet, a former rock musician, a lifelong bachelor with permanently long hair, the big beard, rings on every finger, arms covered in tattoos. And me, the relatively normcore dad, clean-shaven, close-cropped, awkward in a pair of old running shoes.

·

At our dinners, the conversations will inevitably find their way to writing at some point, and on one such occasion a while back I was telling Moralis about the state of my book, worrying yet again about the seemingly intractable nature of its deepest and most difficult subject matter. How there were no clean answers to be found, no conventionally satisfying endings or reassuring epiphanies to hand people.

Not that I'm trying for a fairytale, I said. But there does need to be some level of redemption. It's just hard to be eloquent about speechlessness.

By then we had both finished a couple of tequilas, and Moralis, who is naturally a bit ethereal in his delivery, had also burned through an entire joint on his own before arriving at the restaurant. There was something admirably feral about him, something wholly unbound to convention, which is why, I think,

I had sought out his company in the first place. For weeks I had been feeling entirely too constricted in my approach—too sober and top-heavy and tied up in thought—and needed a dose of his libertine worldview. I told him as much as we sat there, asking him, exasperated, to help me unlock my own head. The rest of the meal was spent dissecting the particulars of my predicament, the conversation frequently collapsing into laughter, and when things had wrapped up and the bill had been paid, Moralis insisted that I accompany him on a quick errand in the neighborhood. He needed to drop in on an old friend of his, he told me, some guy named Dino who had grown up in the Australian Outback, in New South Wales. I tagged along.

·

Walking down Sunset for a few blocks, we hung a left and soon arrived at Dino's house on Lucile Avenue, a smallish Craftsman on a corner lot, badly dilapidated—so much so, in fact, that it appeared as if no one had lived there in years. The curtains all drawn. The lawn overgrown. Not even a porch light burning out front. More than once I asked Moralis if this was some kind of prank, and each time he assured me that it wasn't. To my eyes it looked as if the place had been left for dead, but as soon as we opened the gate and began to make our formal approach, there was the sound of a dog barking ferociously inside. The front door swung open, and there stood Dino, a very bald, very energetic Aussie of indeterminate age who was holding by the collar a very large, very hostile-seeming albino Doberman Pinscher.

This is Gerta, he said to me. She's friendly.

And indeed she was, though it took her a couple of minutes to acclimate to our presence. In all my life, I have never been around a more visually striking dog, a 150-lb., chalk-white Doberman with ice blue eyes and a decidedly needy demeanor. Together, Moralis and I stepped inside and stood in Dino's darkened living room, where it appeared as though he had been snorting cocaine in solitude while watching, of all things, *Sleepless in Seattle.* There was the requisite small mirror laid out on the coffee table, a pile of white power, a credit card, a rolled-up twenty, the open bindle. And on the flat-screen, Tom Hanks now stood frozen, paused, one eye open, mid-conversation, on his dock at Puget Sound. Dino, meanwhile, was talking a mile a minute, standing just a foot away from me, so close that I could smell the beer on his breath. He was a thin-hipped man, hugely friendly in the Australian manner, probably pushing fifty, with a bit of a boxer's nose, some patchy facial hair, deep creases at the corners of his eyes— the look of a wiry featherweight who had lost far more than he'd won.

Taken together—the house, the dog, the coke, the movie—I found myself feeling disoriented in time. It was the most quintessentially Los Angeles experience that I'd had in ages. Moralis followed Dino into the kitchen, out of sight, the two men bantering enthusiastically about a music festival I'd never heard of before, a series of concerts happening out in the desert—not Coachella, but one of its smaller and more intimate offshoots. Meanwhile I remained stationary in the living room, not far from the door, having some one-on-one time with Gerta, whose snout was now lodged firmly into my crotch. The circumstances both amused me and, with every passing second, had me increasingly eager to flee. The house on its own was unnerving, to say nothing of the fact that I now had a large white Doberman—the canine equivalent of cocaine—fixated on my midsection. It was hard to know how to turn her attention elsewhere. Should I take her by the collar? Use my hands? Issue some kind of verbal command? There was the inescapable sense that if I made a false move and somehow triggered a fear response, things could turn ugly in a hurry.

Fortunately, though, it never came to that. I endured all discomforts, kept the dog on an even keel, and a few minutes later was standing outside on the avenue with Moralis, relieved to be in one piece and breathing the jasmine air.

Nice to meet your neighbor, I said. I almost got a bj

from his dog.

Moralis, laughing quietly, pressed a plastic bag into my chest and said, For you.

For a moment I thought he was trying to give me cocaine, which would have been laughable, but when I stepped into the glow of a streetlamp and observed the contents more closely, I could see that the bag was filled with a significant quantity of psilocybin mushrooms.

Well, I said.

I think what you need to do, Moralis told me, in an approximated Australian accent, is wipe the old hard drive clean.

I let out a small laugh and could feel myself shrug. Considering the volume of complaints that I had lodged over dinner, it was hard to argue with the notion.

More than two decades had passed since I'd had any kind of psychedelic experience, the last one happening out in Moab, in college, on the night that I'd gotten my border collie, Merlin. I'd never had any kind of bad trip, but that, I knew, had more to do with luck than anything else. And while I counted these adventures as among the most impactful of my life, there was also a sense of uneasiness about them, a recognition of how haphazard it had all been, how reckless and uninformed, experiences born of sloppy courage and the common foolishness of youth. In the intervening years, I had done a fair bit of reading on the subject and was left with a combination of curiosity and regret.

There was a sincere desire to try it all again, to conduct a proper do-over and take these things "the right way," with a more educated perspective, but up until now all such inklings had lived in the realm of abstraction.

Tucking the bag into one of my coat pockets, I offered Moralis my thanks and assured him that I would take some soon—though I couldn't make any promises about when, exactly, considering the various demands of my domestic and professional lives. Moralis, now puffing a cigarette, seemed unconcerned. Waving a bejeweled hand, he assured me that I would sort out all necessary details, and together we left it at that, walking the short distance back down to Sunset, where I called for a Lyft in a strip mall parking lot. My ride pulled up to the curb a few minutes later, a white Prius with its flashers on, classical music blaring, an older gentleman at the wheel. Moralis bid me farewell with a giant bear hug—a hug so overpowering that my feet came off the ground. He gave me a kiss on the cheek, slapped me on the back, and implored me to go with God. I couldn't help but wonder if he had snorted some of Dino's cocaine.

A COUPLE OF months later, on a Saturday night in January, with Franny's concerned blessing, I took a significant quantity of the mushrooms, alone in the garage. I had made what I felt were careful preparations, using as my basic template the therapeutic research conducted at Johns Hopkins University, one of the only academic institutions in America where the study of psychedelics was legally permitted. Test subjects there were typically dosed, I had learned, in a comfortable, den-like setting, their eyes covered with a sleep mask for the duration. A curated musical playlist, available on Spotify, served as the soundtrack. Under this kind of precise orchestration, and at a measured dose of around three dried grams of mushrooms (suitable for my body weight), genuine mystical experiences were, according to reports, reliably occasioned. My strategy was to try to replicate this arrangement as closely as possible, hoping that it would yield similar results.

It's not like anyone dies, I assured Franny. Statistically it's safer than alcohol, by a long shot. People come out of these experiences feeling better and not worse. They often say it's among the most meaningful things that they've ever done in their lives.

They also have medical staff on hand, she said. And you'll be here with the dog.

•

Franny had been a devoted stoner in her college days but had never developed an interest in anything beyond that. With her sensible Midwestern nature and tendency toward compartmentalization, the prospect of losing psychological control held little appeal, particularly so in the aftermath of Oscar's diagnoses. In her maternal years, she indulged, at most, in a glass or two of Sauvignon Blanc, a vodka soda, the occasional CBD edible. My desire to launch myself into the stratosphere on a sizable dose of mushrooms seemed more than slightly nuts to her, but not altogether unexpected, considering my general temperament and lingering hippie-ish tendencies. I had been talking about doing such a thing, on and off, for the duration of our marriage, the conversation solidifying in recent weeks now that I had some actual product in-hand. Though she had her reservations, I was able to

176

convince her to go along with the plan, assuring her that my approach was scientifically rooted and that every possible precaution would be taken to deliver a smooth ride. Together we decided that she and the kids would drive up to Carpinteria for a long weekend to stay with some friends of ours, so that I could have the house to myself to conduct my experiment.

It's not like you would want to be here anyway, I told her. And obviously I can't do any parenting while I'm in this mode.

What about a friend? she said. Have Mikhail come over.

And do what? I said. Babysit me while I lose my shit for six hours?

Exactly.

I think I'd rather be alone.

And if something goes wrong?

I'll deal with it.

And if you *can't* deal with it?

I'll deal with it anyway.

Right.

What's the worst thing that can happen?

That's exactly what I'm saying!

In that case, I said, I'll be in the fetal position in the garage, in a state of acute psychological distress.

And how is that different from your normal routine?

Ha.

I just don't want to come home, she said, to find you

drooling in the corner, ranting about the CIA.

As if I would drool, I said.

She gave me a look.

I feel confident, I said, raising my right hand. I've done all the reading, and I've got the details nailed down. It'll be fine. And it might even help.

•

On the day of the trip, I stuck to a detailed agenda, working through a list of to-dos in methodical fashion, like an astronaut prepping for a midday launch. In the morning, I took Twiggy on a long hike, as I knew she would be in her crate for several hours. It didn't seem advisable to have her near me while I was under the influence, for fear that it might freak her out, or vice versa. I didn't want to have to worry about her, or be tempted to remove my sleep mask for any reason. The experiment as devised was all about inwardness and the willful elimination of distractions.

There was no breakfast or lunch. Psilocybin only. I had fasted for more than twenty-four hours, in accordance with my research, flushing my system a bit to avoid any digestive upset, and to intensify the effects of the trip. Using a digital scale, I weighed out my dosage precisely, setting the mushrooms in a small bowl, after which I built a kind of makeshift altar on the coffee table, with candles and an orchid and some of my favorite books, and so on. Here again I was following protocol, in an effort to ritualize the proceedings and imbue them with a measure of sacred meaning.

I then turned to my notebook and wrote awhile, jotting down some of my concerns and expectations, as this, too, I had read, could be helpful in tamping down anxieties and setting a general framework for the experience. *I will admit to feeling a bit of fear*, I confessed—

—and can't help but notice that I've been pacing a lot today, wandering from room to room for no particular reason, as if I were searching for something but couldn't remember quite what. At this high of a dose, it seems likely, based on research, that the dissolution of my ego will at some point factor in, an eventuality about which I feel both uneasy and excited in equal measure. Having never been through the process before— my earlier trips were, I'm almost certain, at a far lower dose—it's hard to know what it might entail. Anyway, I'm ready for it (I think?). I've spent more than four decades inside my own head. Bring on the dissolution. But remember to stay calm when things get weird. And they will get weird. And when it happens, just breathe. And when the monsters show up, jump into their mouths. Remember this. Probably the

179

most important guideline. Yield to overcome. So crucial.

My phone, I have decided, will be left inside and powered down. I can't believe I was even debating it. Put the thing away, for godsake. Franny alone knows what I'm up to and I have advised her that there will be no contact until I have emerged. If something goes truly haywire, I've promised to text her, and she'll summon Mikhail or another of our friends to come over and exfiltrate me. Otherwise, I'll be fully incommunicado. Once the trip is underway and I've achieved cruising altitude, there's not much I could do from a responsive standpoint anyway. So for the next five-to-seven hours, I'll be completely off the grid and in orbit.

Am I ready? Of course not.

A fitting final thought before launch.

Om mani padme hum.

P.S. If for some reason I don't make it back: I love you all.

.

As a general rule, psychedelic experiences are incredibly slippery and hard to recollect. They tend to defy language, leaving even the most garrulous of subjects at a loss for words. Whatever it is that transpires is

fundamentally ineffable, often absurd, and demateri-
alizes quickly. In most cases, one is left with, at best,
a stupefying feeling of having lived through something
profound, of having ventured off into an alien realm
of consciousness for which there is no obvious lexicon.

I was aware of all this going into the trip and had
therefore committed myself to a process of written documentation in the immediate aftermath of the experience, knowing that there would be a limited window of
time in which to write down the fleeting particulars.
As soon as I felt even remotely functional, I turned to
my notebook, trying my best to record what had happened in something close to real time. Scribbling in a
slanted and decidedly shaky script, I managed to fill a
couple of pages with the following preliminary reflec-
tions—which, generously speaking, read like the rav-
ings of a lunatic college freshman:

> *I did not expect to be this emotional. I didn't
> expect to see Oprah—so real. I love this room.
> Playing bongos? Appropriate! I did not expect
> to sob so much or experience so many past lives.
> Astonishing.*
>
> *What I kept saying—crying out, almost—as I
> wept: Remarkable!*
>
> *So genuinely amazing to be here. So many
> tears.*
>
> *I swear I became an old man and my voice*

changed. I could feel my body die, get weak and thin. It was okay!

I realize I'm tripping. I'm sitting here on the couch.

I felt Aunt Rosalyn. She was there. Didn't expect it. She was right there. So powerful. I cried so hard. I wish I had met you, Ros. Never knew you but I know you, and I'm glad we said hello.

I felt such a strong connection to the suffering of other human beings, of women and children in particular. All that goodness and love, beaten down by hate. It made me so sad.

I sang. I can't sing a fucking note, but I sang.

I remember weeping as I said, very clearly: I want to help people.

No magic bullets. No shortcuts.

Make music! Make art!

What a trip, right? Jesus. So much I did not expect.

There are dimensions of consciousness that we have only just begun to understand. For a while I felt out-of-body. There was a physical sense of inhabitance in some "next layer," a kind of consciousness super-highway. (I know this sounds insane.)

Career ideas: Shaman. Author of silly books for kids.

I could go for a cigarette.

•

There was no trouble getting the mushrooms down. There had been some mild concern that they might make me sick, but it wasn't an issue. I chewed them to liquid, dealt with the muddy taste, and washed it all down with water. I then sat quietly on the couch and waited, alternately pulling the sleep mask over my eyes and then removing it again, engaging in this fidgety dance for the better part of an hour. The come-on was gradual, nearly undetectable, and at the thirty-minute mark, in a fit of impatience, I ate a few more caps, escalating my total intake to four grams even, worried—absurdly, in retrospect—that the effects weren't going to be strong enough. If I was going to do this, I told myself, I wanted to really do it. No half-measures. Fuck it. I was going all in.

Jittery behavior notwithstanding, the underlying physical sensation throughout was closer to lethargy than to any kind of mania. There was zero desire to run around or be outside or go anywhere—something else I had worried about, thinking that I might, under the influence, make the impulsive decision to leave the house and strike out into the neighborhood on a bug-eyed adventure. I need not have been concerned. Rather than wanting to get up and move, I instead felt plastered to the couch, triple my own body weight, entirely content to remain in place and listen to music—a notable departure from the more kinetic trips of my youth, most of which took place at crowded house parties and packed stadium concerts.

At around the forty-five minute mark, I thought I could detect an initial lift, a gentle but significant high, and by the time I crossed over into the second hour, I was fully on my back and behind my eyelids. What appeared were a succession of images, colors, faces, thoughts, a mental landscape not dissimilar to the earliest stages of sleep, kaleidoscopic in its expression. The Johns Hopkins playlist was helpful in bringing me along, expertly curated for mood and meaning, and as the trip intensified I kept laughing at how suggestible I was to every song change, my internal field of vision moving in concert with the music.

As the experience continued to materialize, my mind space began to morph into something more visually sophisticated, taking on a distinct three-dimensional quality. The archetypal swirling patterns gave way to an actual physical environment, and I was surprised to find myself weaving through a crowded outdoor marketplace, an elaborate bazaar of some kind, the location of which seemed vaguely South American in its aesthetic. Wandering the aisles, taking it all in, I spotted for the first time a beautiful woman, indigenous in her appearance—but only at a distance, and fleetingly. She seemed to be beckoning me to follow her, but all efforts to do so were repeatedly thwarted by the crowd. Every time I made a turn or tried to move forward in pursuit, the congestion would intensify, closing in around me, delivering a suffocating effect, causing me to feel a sense of despair—but then, after a time, as if by magic, the entire scene dispersed, mutating instantly, giving way to a beautiful forest, where, liberated, I continued in my quest to find the mysterious woman, who kept appearing in flashes up ahead, disappearing into the trees, a kind of prankster tour guide, leading me into the depths of my trip.

I don't recall ever catching up with her and feel reasonably sure that I did not. What remains in my memory is the futile pursuit, followed by an astonishing succession of pyrotechnic mental events of extraordinary power and strangeness. I remember it only in pieces but can say with confidence that sometime after arriving in the trees I was launched, very deeply, into a mind-blowing trance, an hours-long surge of thought and image and feeling, overpowering in every sense of the term, both real and surreal, and maddeningly hard to reconstruct as any kind of cohesive narrative.

A central feature of this phase involved, stunningly, the distinct presence of destitute people from another time: men, women, and children dressed in rags, many of them emaciated or visibly ill. It seemed clear to me that they were slaves or prisoners of some kind, and as I looked into their eyes a powerful wave of sorrow rose up within me and bloomed in my chest like a flower. In

my psychedelic field of vision these people were posi-
tioned below, a large group of them packed down into a
muddy hole, gazing up from what seemed to be a mass
grave. As I stood there looking at them, and they at
me, I felt an extraordinary sense of connection and recognition, as if I knew them all deeply, at a DNA level,
and vice versa. However absurd it may sound, there
was not an ounce of contrivance to it. All pure.

The next thing I recall, I was down inside the
grave myself, packed in with everyone, locked among
the limbs and torsos, barely able to move. And as I
lay there with my eyes open, the bodies around me
slowly became corpses, and I was presented with all
of the visible grotesqueries of flesh: slime and guts
and deformed and decomposing faces, everything
happening in time-lapse, death in all of its majesty, a
rapid transition to dust. And strangely, I could handle
it just fine. No problems, no sense of fear or revulsion,
no strong desire to escape. And no real surprise, either.
It was as though I had fully expected this to happen,
had ventured down inside this grave for exactly this
purpose and was calmly confronting the ravages of
time so that I might better understand my own fate.
And after everyone else had died, I myself began to
die, my body undergoing its rapid decomposition, the
presence of my own skeleton announcing itself inside
my skin. It was so extraordinary, it caused me to gasp. I
said something aloud here—I forget exactly what—but

do remember clearly that my voice was the voice of an old man, and this, I knew, was precisely what I would sound like on my deathbed. The air of cosmic neutrality with which I was carrying myself struck me even then as fundamentally strange. The fact that I was dying and didn't really mind—how incredible. And at the same time so utterly normal. Of course it was no big deal. Birth and death, happening every second, in every corner of the world. The cells in my body perishing and regenerating constantly, without me even realizing it, an ongoing, mutual process rather than a single cataclysmic event.

And when the ritual of my own disintegration had finished, I then began to experience resurrection, feeling myself *become* a series of different individuals, women mostly, seemingly from long ago, inhabiting their bodies—this was the overwhelming sensation of it—as if I were a ghost revisiting past lives, one after the other, moving through a number of manifestations, like I was trying on old clothes. I had read about such things during my research phase, stories of people experiencing cross-cultural and cross-gendered connectivity while under the influence, including William Burroughs and Allen Ginsberg, who had reported similar happenings in *The Yagé Letters.*

Eventually I emerged into a crowded room filled with people and old furniture, and I myself was embodied as a Black woman at this point, all of us hugging one another in sadness and solidarity. And it was in the midst of all this hugging that I emerged from my trance just enough to realize that I was weeping behind my sleep mask. A very faint level of tangible physical awareness at the periphery, a slowly-returning sense of self. And as the fact of my weeping began to solidify, my appearance inside the trip reverted to the norm. My female identity fell away like a coat dropping to the floor, and I was suddenly myself again, alive inside the phantasm, Brad the Sad Dad, sobbing and hugging my comrades in this strange room, a three-dimensional participant in a shockingly vivid dream that had now become lucid. At this point I was hugging a woman tightly, an experience of incredible tactile realness, so much so that I could smell the shampoo in her hair. And as the sensory awareness intensified, I pulled away a bit so as to look at the woman's face, and when I did I found myself eye-to-eye, unmistakably, with Oprah Winfrey, who told me with great enthusiasm to let my feelings flow (*Let it go, baby!* I remember her saying), an encouragement that caused me to both explode in laughter and bawl my eyes out at the same time.

.

And here I must make an obligatory acknowledgment of how utterly batshit insane this all sounds. At least, I tell myself, I too was laughing by this point, marginally aware of how nuts things had become. A full-grown man, alone in his garage, blindfolded, flat on his back, bawling his eyes out on mushrooms, having an Oprah moment. And yet for all of the inherent absurdity, the emotional release was authentic and overwhelming in the extreme. It was as though some kind of floodgate had been opened inside of me, and every ounce of sadness that I had ever felt or buried or intuited or witnessed from afar came pouring out of my body in a massive deluge. For nearly three solid hours, I lay there on the couch, crying like an absolute baby, powerless to stop it. I wept for myself and my former selves, for Oscar and Alice and Franny, for suffering creatures the world over, the infirm and the destitute and the insane, and for America, and for my parents and sisters, and for my aunts and uncles and cousins and friends, for my ancestors and for Oprah, for every plant and animal in the entire stupid universe. I wept like it was my job. I wept to the point of dehydration. I pulled my sleep mask away from my eyes and wept for the garage too, for the altar and the orchid and the candles, all of it. I wept until I didn't have anything left to weep for anymore. And then I kept on weeping.

.

At some point, I pulled the mask back over my eyes and as the tears continued to fall I began to hallucinate again, another wave of immersion. It was here that my

Aunt Rosalyn appeared from out of nowhere—except I couldn't quite see her. There were fleeting images only, similar to the indigenous woman in the forest from earlier in the trip. Rather than manifesting in a stable human form, there was instead an astonishing sense of her disembodied presence at close range. Within my field of vision I could see a ball of bright white light, and within it she was *there*, and I knew it beyond a shadow of a doubt. It was clear that she was communicating with me from another realm, saying hello. And though there was no conversation in conventional terms, I could sense that she was telling me to live for her, to go all the way, to really enjoy my time, which caused me to weep even more. By this point I had a Kleenex in my hand, having pulled it from my pocket, and had blown my nose so many times that the tissue was practically disintegrated. Again I removed the sleep mask and looked around the room and laughed aloud at the unbelievable state of things, and what an absolute sniveling mess I was, lost inside this unprecedented purge. The only thing I could think to say in response to it all was: *remarkable.* Over and over and over again: *remarkable.* Looking down at the little headless skeleton on the altar, repeating it aloud, as if it were the only word in the universe that made any sense at all. *Remarkable. Remarkable. Remarkable.*

·

Another thing I remember saying toward the tail end of the trip: *I did not expect that.* An entirely rational response, considering that so much of what transpired had come as an absolute shock. Going into it, there had been zero thoughts of Rosalyn. Not a single one. Oprah was not on my radar—at all—nor had I been thinking about oppressed peoples throughout history, or the possibility of past lives. If anything, I was concerned that I would fixate on Oscar and Alice and get lost in a downward spiral of paternal guilt and sorrow, or that my buddies who had died prematurely in a self-destructive manner would emerge from the ether and accuse me of being an inattentive friend. It was this sort of thing about which I had been most fearful, but in the end it wasn't a problem. While I did think of Franny and the kids at several turns, it never created even the slightest bit of difficulty for me. If anything it served as a kind of anchoring device, a reminder of all that was good and immoveable and true.

.

From my notebook, later that night:

> *No major revelations to report with regard to practical matters, no big breakthroughs creatively or career-wise, no total vanquishing of my heartbreak over Oscar, or anything along these lines. The most I could come up with was the phrase "no*

magic bullets, no shortcuts," which I remember incanting to myself a handful of times in the middle of the trip, a platitude that arrived with the force of a mind-blowing epiphany.

The experience, it seems clear, wasn't about tidy resolutions but was instead, more than anything else, about the physical expression of a deep, internalized sadness, a sadness far larger and more repressed than I had previously understood. And to think that all this time I had conceived of myself as a man in tune with his own interior. How farcical. My confusion reigns. I am always and forever blind.

The mushrooms, if nothing else, facilitated an enormous grief experience, a spectacular flood of feeling that I never could've mustered on my own. It isn't that I didn't know that I was sad—of course I knew. (Everyone is sad.) But until I had this experience, I had never been allowed, or had never allowed myself, to feel the full measure of it in any kind of embodied way. Probably also a matter of simple logistics. To get this sad, and to cry this hard, requires intense concentration. Most reasonably sane adults would need, I think, some serious assistance and a small, quiet room.

My eyes are incredibly raw right now. They actually burn. Sore to the touch. I imagine they're red. Some blood vessels might've burst. I haven't looked at myself yet. It would be impossible to overstate just how much I wept over the past few hours. Unexpected and completely outrageous. And it wasn't only my sadness over Oscar that I was feeling, either—it went far beyond that, extending to everything and everyone. The extraordinary hugeness of it all. To experience at the cellular level the deep interconnectedness of all people and things across space and time, to be brought into some kind of intimate communion with the enormous love that binds the universe. Is this what happened to me? (I think this is what happened to me?) I touched it, or it touched me—the unity experience that all religions suggest?—or maybe I was just really fucking high and my serotonin receptors were firing out of control. Whatever the case, it hit me like a freight train, but at the point of impact it was more like the touch of a feather. And when it happened, all I could do was weep. On this level, and in accordance with my reading, it's hard not to view the experience as having been genuinely mystical in nature, or as close as I've ever come to encountering such a thing.

.

Credit to the researchers at Johns Hopkins University, I texted Franny a while later. *Those motherfuckers know what they're talking about.*

Glad you're alive, was her initial reply. She included several mushroom emojis, along with a couple of unicorns, followed by: *One sec.* And then, about a minute after that: *How do you feel?*

Bush did 9/11, I said.

Ha.

For much of the next hour, I attempted to recount all that had happened, typing it out on my phone, line by line. I didn't have it in me to talk just yet and wanted to add to my archive of written documentation while the memories were fresh.

It sounds so utterly silly when you put it down, I said. *Just a thunderclap of an experience. Amazingly life-affirming and entirely bananas. And the whole "dying and resurrecting" sequence. WTF. I was actually, like, inside the bodies of these people, I swear to god. Out of nowhere. A complete shock. How does one explain such a thing? I can only imagine that I was experiencing some deep form of connectivity or bearing witness to past lives or working out some kind of ancestral guilt or something. I'm also now remembering that at one point I locked in very powerfully on why people make music and sing. I started laughing and singing as I was lying there, and felt this incredibly deep understanding of the origins of music and how it is related to human suffering.*

Please don't post online about any of this, Franny said.

SOME TIME LATER, well after sundown, with a full moon rising in the eastern sky, I retrieved Twiggy from her crate, letting her into the yard. I sat on a lawn chair in the driveway, feeling myself breathe. I stared at the moon for a while, listening to the distant traffic sounds, then rose from my chair and went inside, where I drank a couple of liters of water at the sink and cut up a large pineapple with a butcher knife. The house was silent, eerily so, the kids' toys at rest, the living room dimly lit. There was a distinct strangeness to being alone in this space, a space so typically frenetic and filled with life, as if I were a ghost haunting my own house. Standing over the cutting board, famished, I wolfed down the entire pineapple in a matter of minutes, then went into the bathroom and peed and washed my hands, looking at myself in the mirror for the first time, post-trip. The continued dilation of my pupils, the distinct redness of my sclera, the healthy-looking pallor of my skin. I made a variety of faces at myself, gave myself the finger, then returned to the driveway and texted a brief summary of my day to Mikhail, emphasizing that the trip had been positive despite all the ludicrous weeping.

Truly transcendent, was his immediate response. *Beauteous, Mr. Brad. I'm so glad les champignons took you to the good and opening place. We don't cry enough because we're warriors. But spiritual warriors need to cry the tears of the world every once in a while. Mucho love, mio fratello.*

.

For the next hour or so, I sat at the patio table with a pen in-hand, alternately stupefied and scribbling into my notebook. By the time I finished the entry, I had filled about six pages. It was well after 10:00 PM. There were no thoughts of going to bed or watching television or winding down or doing anything domestically typical. Though my body was weary, sleep felt a long way off, my mind continuing to hum with residual chemical energy, a kind of restless limbo. I didn't really want to be indoors, nor did I want to talk with anyone. The only thing I could think to do was to take Twiggy for a walk, armed with whatever new perspective I had gained.

Together we exited the house, moving southward,

aimlessly, out across the flats. I was struck almost immediately by how garish and alien everything seemed, the neon storefronts, the 7-Eleven, the whir of traffic, the smell of pot smoke wafting from an apartment building. All of it somehow new again, obnoxious in interesting ways. To think that there were millions of people huddled under this one patch of sky. The weirdness and magic and misery of that. Modern civilization and its repeating patterns, its obscene levels of hyperactivity. And how far away from it all I had been just a few hours ago, how utterly divorced from reality in its conventional guise. *Right back into the thick of it,* I thought, grinning a little. And how convincing it all appeared, how solid and fixed and concrete, when in fact every single speck of it, every last person and animal and insect and blade of grass, every window pane and streetlight and palm tree and hedgerow would be rendered into dust motes in a cosmic minute. My death experience on mushrooms had shown me as much in Technicolor. And probably, I thought, this was the most valuable part of the whole thing. The supreme nonchalance with which I had greeted my own demise. Whatever had happened to me in the midst of all that, I didn't want to lose it. As much as I possibly could, I hoped to retain that sense of cool, that firm connection to my own emptiness, attuned to the scales of time. A few blinks ago, I had been a boy in Milwaukee, ice-skating on a frozen creek, playing hockey, wandering through the woods with my buddies, in search of arrowheads. And soon enough, with some luck, I would be a tired old man, mottled and wheezing, careening toward infinity, wondering what the hell had happened to age forty-two. I could expect no less.

.

A police chopper thwumped across the sky, headed southeast in the direction of downtown, its taillight blinking in a cardiac rhythm. As I watched it disappear into the night, I passed in front of a gourmet ice cream shop, outside of which stood a mass of people, almost all of whom were of adult age, many with their cones in-hand. An increasingly common sight in Los Angeles. Little artisan ice cream shops popping up everywhere. Nearly every time I ventured out, it seemed like I was confronted with a herd of yuppies eating ice cream with basil in it or something. A kind of stress response, I told myself. Poetic and sad. Ice cream as a symbol of mortality, an obvious relic of childhood—and it was melting. There was something tragic about the entire charade, something infantilizing and grim, a bunch of grown men and women comforting themselves with the culinary equivalent of crack cocaine, walking around with their frozen sugar treats, licking at their cones like sad wild animals—and here I started giggling aloud, surprised by the fluid intensity of my thinking, the complete morbid certainty of my conclusions. Had I just witnessed a bunch of advanced apes hanging on to their sanity by their fingernails, trying desperately to crawl back inside the womb? Or were they simply some nice people out on a Saturday night, enjoying ice cream cones? It felt hard to say. Maybe both were true. And probably I wasn't as sober as I thought I was.

•

For the rest of my walk, I continued in this vein, unable to look at anything without taking it apart. Every single billboard in town was, I decided, abominably ugly. Terrible eyesores in every direction, pretending to be art, vicious little monuments to insincerity. The fact that we tolerated this ugliness—pathetic. And as I passed by a school, it occurred to me that in all my years of education, there had been no substantive conversation around death as a practical matter. Absolutely none. And how criminally insane this seemed. And how the nervous energy of Los Angeles felt easy to understand in this context, a place where death had been relegated to the shadows, youth had been turned into a virtue, and a person's image was often more important than her reality. No wonder people maintained a religious devotion to their distractions, bottled up inside their cars—cars which, at a functional level, were essentially just giant phones that spit poison into the atmosphere while they ferried you about town, advertising to you, tracking your whereabouts, collecting your data. And on it went.

·

By the time I arrived back home, it was well after midnight. I went upstairs and took a hot shower, then climbed into bed and was out within minutes. I had been hoping for an epic night of sleep, but just four hours later I snapped awake again, as if a switch had been flipped, feeling strangely refreshed and a little bit cotton-headed. Blinking at the ceiling, I lay there for a long moment, hoping I might drift, but soon enough it became apparent that my body had a different agenda. Whatever restlessness had possessed me the night before was still working its way out of my system. I got up.

After splashing some cold water on my face, I peed and brushed my teeth and decided, somewhat absurdly, to go for another walk, to continue where I had left off, feeling that I should treat the day normally and get some exercise first thing. A man of routines. I needed to equalize, to ready my head for the return of Franny and the kids, who were due back from Carpinteria sometime after lunch. It felt important that I not betray even the slightest bit of a hangover.

If I appeared zombie-eyed in any way, looking like I'd blown a fuse, it would undermine the credibility of my experiment, calling my judgment into question. Better to power through it, I felt. Better to atone, to get some fresh air and work myself into a flop sweat.

With the sky still dark, I set out on foot with Twiggy, marching her up to Griffith Park, where we began our ascent into the hills just before 7:00 AM. Our usual winding route. Three or four mornings a week we did this together, from Beachwood Canyon to the trailhead, up beyond the Hollywood sign, to the summit of Mt. Lee. One of the principle virtues of Los Angeles, I had long felt, was the accessibility of mountain trails within city limits, a real American rarity. The fact that an actual mountain lion made its home inside the park only added to the appeal. The lion, a solitary male named P-22, was a bit of a celebrity in town. Years ago, he had made the unlikely journey from the western flank of the Santa Monica range, across the 101 and 405 Freeways into the park's eight-square-mile expanse. Through the years, I had hiked within its boundaries hundreds of times, almost always at sunrise—a prime hunting hour for any large cat. I had seen dozens of coyotes, raccoons, hawks, rabbits, a handful of deer, but never once had I laid eyes on P-22, even at a distance. Cougars are notoriously elusive, not at all likely to interact with humans, but still I couldn't help but wonder, as Twiggy and I made our ascent in the predawn dark, if P-22 was somewhere nearby, tracking my every footfall and planning a sudden ambush.

There was some small part of me that liked the possibility of being eaten alive, liked how the stakes were raised by the presence of this cat, a creature that arguably transformed the city itself into a legitimate wilderness, redeeming it on some level. It was astonishing to think that a large mammalian predator was allowed to roam inside a city park that played host to more than five million people annually. And yet the coexistence had been entirely successful so far, continuing for years without incident. P-22 appeared to have no appetite for human flesh. *Then again,* I thought, *appearances can change.* And maybe today would be the day. Maybe this would be my narrative. The capstone of the entire crazy weekend. *Man stays home alone, eats a mother lode of mushrooms, sobs for hours, cries the tears of the world, and the next morning, at dawn, is devoured by a lion in an urban park.* I could think of worse ways to go out. Both Twiggy and I would be mauled. We would perish together, P-22 dragging our bodies one by one into the underbrush, feasting upon our organs over a period of days. The Tongva people, native inhabitants of the Los Angeles basin, believed that lions were an omen-bearing species, likely to appear in times of spiritual crisis. Occasionally they would avenge Mother Nature. Fair enough. Perhaps, I thought,

Twiggy and I would be the sacrificial lambs, our bodies disappeared into the earth, never to be found. The mystery would linger for decades, torturing my poor family, but eventually, like all things, it would fade away into nothingness. At some point in the not-too-distant future, my name would be spoken aloud for the very last time, and in that precise instant the finality of my passing would become eternal.

•

Cresting a ridge, breathing heavily, I arrived at a full view of the city's expanse, the streetlights still twinkling, the sun just beginning to fracture the eastern horizon. There it was, the big mess of it, spread out like a bed of diamonds, disappearing into the desert. It was an absolutely terrible place, and I loved it. A city of infinite lunacy, the embodiment of everything that was right and wrong with the world. And how many people down there were sleeping right now? And how many were fucking? How many were tripping on mushrooms, crying into the palms of their hands? How many were dying lonely deaths or making music or praying to the sky? How many rats were crawling around in the alleyways? How many babies were being born? The scale of it, so ridiculous, a byzantine organism sprung from scorched earth in under two hundred years.

Turning back to the trail, I resumed my ascent, and

soon caught sight of a man headed toward me, coming down from the summit in a blue hooded sweatshirt. I recognized him immediately. Though I didn't know his name, I had seen him dozens, if not hundreds of times. Anyone who hiked this early tended to do so on a regular basis. A kind of urban tribe. For years I had been passing the same rotation of weirdos. The man in question was probably in his sixties, a burly, silver-haired brute who almost never made eye contact, and who strangely, for reasons unexplained, hiked to the top of Mt. Lee most mornings with a football tucked under his arm. There was nothing otherwise "off" about him, no obvious signs of mental disturbance, but he did always give the distinct impression of being in a terrible hurry, and of not wanting to talk with anyone. I had never even bothered trying. Dawn hikers tended to respect the solitude of other dawn hikers. To me, the man's taciturn nature and focused intensity were part of his appeal. In my head, I had always referred to him as Mr. Football, another quintessential Los Angeles character, fending off insanity with his rituals.

On this day, however, as we passed each other, there was a brief moment of eye contact, and I heard myself offer him a good morning. The man slowed his pace a bit, a little wild-eyed, and looked back at me. We're here on the mountain, he said, and gave me a nod. He then pointed over my shoulder, in the direction of the eastern horizon, and told me, before continuing on his way: Looks like we've got a wildfire.

I turned. The sun was now fully visible in the lowest reaches of the sky, casting the hillsides in a brilliant orange light. Far out in the distance, I was able to see for the first time a wildfire burning in the hills above Glendora, sending up a thick black plume. It was January and wildfires weren't supposed to be burning, but the winter, which was supposed to be the rainy season, had once again been alarmingly dry and summer-like, and the fires had continued to spark.

As I made my way up to the summit, the size of the blaze came into clearer view, the plume rising higher into the atmosphere and dispersing, the flames pulsing on the distant hills. The morning sky was extraordinary, a magnificent arrangement of cirrus clouds awash in bursts of color, big gold beams of sunlight refracted through the pollution. A small crowd had gathered on the road above the Hollywood sign, everyone marveling at the show, and in particular at a big brown cloud that had drifted out over the city like a flying saucer, an entirely unnatural-looking formation, massive and iridescent in the sunlight, its contours aglow in neon pink. People were taking pictures of it with their cell phones. I took a few myself.

What is it? a woman next to me said.

Smog, I told her. It's beautiful.

FRANNY AND THE kids didn't return home until early evening, pulling into the driveway just as the sun was going down. The weather in Carpinteria had been gorgeous. They had stayed on through the afternoon, playing at the beach, Franny figuring I would need some time to recover. She wasn't wrong. I napped from eleven to two, starfished on our bed, then woke and did the grocery shopping for the week, wandering through Trader Joe's with my headphones on, listening to Claude Debussy at high volume. Dinner was ready when they came through the door, a big Italian feast, spaghetti and salad and garlic bread. Music playing. Candles lit. Wine. Everything in its place. An elegant performance of normalcy. They had been gone for only thirty-six hours, but it felt like far longer. The relief of having them home. A restoration of the natural order.

Everyone looking healthy, new, tinged with an earthy glow, fresh from a day in the sun, breathing all that sea air. Oscar tottered across the floor and hugged my leg and said, I missed you, Daddy. Alice wanted to know what I had done in their absence. I told her I had worked, which on some level was true. From the start, my remaining behind in Los Angeles had been presented as a matter of professional necessity.

What did you work on? she wanted to know.

I worked on myself, I said, trying not to lie.

My answer didn't satisfy her.

Yeah, she said, but what was your *job*?

I'm a writer, I told her. You know that. And a podcaster. And a . . . creative consultant content professional.

As the words left my mouth, I could feel myself wincing internally. The absurd complexities of my working life, with all of its tiresome hyphenations and blurry lines. Everything subject to change.

Yeah, she said. But what were you actually *doing*?

I explained that I had been working on an audio project—also true—though I hadn't given it a single thought since Friday. Another installment of the "iconic American food products" series. The latest episode was all about the Slim Jim.

Alice didn't know what a Slim Jim was. I attempted to explain it to her. She made a face.

That sounds boring, she said.

I laughed. I could hardly disagree. An audio documentary about beef jerky. My life's work.

I also interview writers for my podcast, I said, trying to redeem myself. And I'm working on a book of my own.

This last item caused her face to brighten. What kind of book? she wanted to know.

It's not entirely clear, I said.

Is it for kids?

I don't think so.

Well, what's it about? she said.

I'm still trying to decide.

Again she made a face.

It's about you, I told her.

Really?

You could say that.

That's exciting! she said.

It might be.

What happens in it? What do I do?

A lot of things probably. I'm still sorting it out. I'll let you know when it's done.

She sat there sizing me up, twirling some noodles on her fork.

So what else happened while we were gone? she said.

I climbed a mountain, I told her.

Really?

Yeah.

Which one?
The same one I always climb.
How big is it?
About two thousand feet.
That's big.
It's actually not that big.
Two thousand feet is small?
When it comes to mountains it is.
She thought it over.
I have a question, she said.
Sure. Go ahead.
How big is the smallest mountain in the world?

•

After the dishes were rinsed and put away and the kids had been bathed, I tucked Oscar in, lying next to him in his bed, reading him a picture book about monster trucks. He started to doze almost immediately, exhausted from his day at the beach, and by the time I turned the final page he was out cold.

Rolling off of his mattress as quietly as I could, I knelt on the rug at his bedside and put my face up close to his and listened to him breathe. The gentle wheeze of his exhalations. The soapy smell of his hair, still wet from the bath. Touching my nose to his, I took in some of his kid breath, then closed my eyes and clasped my hands together and said my nightly prayer, asking that the gods heal him and keep him safe, that his future be filled with laughter and love and deep purpose.

There was always an element of self-consciousness to the ritual, the goofy-headed sense that I didn't really know to whom or what I was praying. And still I did it, night after night, with a real measure of devotion. Hedging my bets. The irony of the apostate on his knees. It only ever happened when I was tucking my kids in, or when I was on an airplane and the engines were firing before takeoff. Almost everyone, I tended to believe, resorted to prayer at times like these, whether they admitted to it or not. For me it was less about direct communication and more an act of quiet surrender to the vast incomprehensibility and deep precariousness of it all. A confession of my own weakness and the wish that the hands of fate might spare my family from any further tragedies. *No más.* There in the darkness, with my son drifting off, the limits of my control always seemed particularly plain. The fragility of this boy. The fragility of us all. Where else was I supposed to go in the face of it, other than down on my knees?

•

In recent years, whenever the subject of God came up, my answer to Alice was always the same: God is everything. That was it. A simple, three-word explanation, one with which I could live, one that felt honest enough without being too damnably bleak. The idea was to keep it benign, nonpunitive, non-patriarchal, to put it in terms she could understand, and to pass along a basic spirit of reverence—not just for all of the beauty in the world, and the astonishing mysteries of the cosmos—but for all of the ugliness too.

You're God, I would tell her. I'm God. The sky is God. The moon is God. Even the garbage is God.

Is poop God?

Poop is God.

She would laugh.

Why are smelly things God?

You can't grow flowers without smelly things.

Is Chickie God?

Chickie was her favorite stuffed animal, a small, yellow stuffed chick that she had been attached to since she was a toddler.

Chickie is most definitely God.

And so on.

•

There was always a certain eagerness to escape these conversations, to get out before I did any damage. On this front, I had learned my lesson. *Short and sweet or keep your mouth shut.* The challenge of delivering ready answers to impossible questions, of dealing in both nuance and kid-speak simultaneously. I wasn't any good at it. Always second-guessing everything, wondering if I should've been blunter, ultimately opting for a simple definition, equating the word "God" with a general sense of awe. To me, the darker alternatives had always felt too pitiless, too religious, too sure of their own strength—God is nothing, God doesn't exist, the universe is an infinite vacuum of terrifying emptiness—and anyway, I didn't believe it. Not fully. My experiences in life had given me at least some cause for wonder. Just yesterday, in fact, I'd been awash in the holiness of Mushroom Land, with all of its past lives and virginal noticing and dissolving into oneness, the sacred dimensions of ordinary experience brought into high relief. None of it could be easily squared with a hyper-rational worldview. What I seemed to have learned, again, emphatically, was that I knew almost nothing at all. *Amen.* Reality was weird as fuck. *Hallelujah.* A magnificent puzzle, not at all absent of magic. And while the mystery was well worth exploring, as I knelt there at Oscar's bedside, I was engaged, it seemed, in an act of concession, an acknowledgement that there were limits to the enterprise. Hands clasped, eyes closed, head empty—this was where my prayers tended to leave me. Aware that the puzzle could never be solved. Not by me, anyway. *No magic bullets, no shortcuts.* For all of my kneeling and praying, Oscar's disability wasn't likely to change. My understanding wasn't likely to crystallize into some kind of infinite bliss. There would never be a single guarantee.

.

It wasn't that I didn't have hope. I had plenty of it. Advancements in medicine were happening every day. And maybe there would be a supernatural response to physical therapy—a defiant, miraculous healing—who knew? This stuff happened sometimes. But to focus too much on such things was, I told myself, a misallocation of time. To get too lost in the wishing was, again, to miss the real miracle, the simple fact that Oscar and I were here at all, in whatever form, and for whatever reasons, the two of us together in this room, breathing the same crazy air. The job was not to mourn over his existence, or wish that he were some way other than he was. The job was to be his dad, simple as that, and to take care of him and celebrate him, exactly as is—Alice and Franny too—to appreciate them all, for however long this tenuous arrangement lasted. That was it. Period. Nothing more. *Enjoy it, dumbass. The rest is details. Just enjoy. Forget about trying to have a better past, and accept that some questions have no answers. The answer is that there are no answers. And that's the only answer there will ever be.*

My son had sustained a wound and his wound was my wound and the abnormality of the wound had to do with its timing. To be wounded from birth: unlucky. A brain injury: difficult. But disability was no rare thing. It was everywhere. In the aftermath of Oscar's diagnoses, it was as though blinders had been removed from my eyes. All of these people in the streets with their walkers and canes and hearings aids and prosthetic limbs. They seemed to have appeared out of nowhere, but of course they had been there all along, waiting for me. And eventually I would become one of them. Any day now, really. Tomorrow I could fall ill, knocked back by some disease, relegated to my bed—disabled. An injury might do it. A shattered leg. A broken spine. A psychiatric condition. And if none of that did the trick, then aging most certainly would. Disability was not only normal, it was inevitable. It was simply a matter of where you existed on the continuum. One of Oscar's primary challenges would involve making peace with his starting point, to see it less as a mark of difference and more as a binding thread. Was it unfair? Hell yes, it was unfair. And what were we to do about the unfairness? Try to learn from it. That was it. Try to learn how to learn from it. And accept its hard embrace.

·

The miseries and the beauties of life, in all of their transitory majesty. Nothing great. Everything small. Everything forgotten over time. Every victory. Every defeat. Every love. Every grief. Every wound. All of it obliterated, before too long. The agony and the ecstasy of it, rolled into one. When everything was working out fine, it could be easy to accept the idea of destiny. It could be easy to fall into magical thinking, and to talk about feeling blessed. You might even discount the notion of luck, or find yourself buying into the idea that everything was ultimately positive in the celestial scheme of things, and whatever hardships might come along, they would only serve to make you a better person, if you just developed the right attitude. But when the shit really hit the fan—when it happened to you and yours—good luck trying to see it as anything other than treachery and violation and hideous misfortune. The crude mechanics of calamity, when they were really bearing down on you, were something to behold. Those hard, dark, lonely moments when you realized how totally defeated you were, how heart-shattered and boxed-in and mortal, unable to escape. The future becoming something alien in the blink of an eye. Maybe, if you were made of stronger stuff, lucky and surrounded by love, you could emerge from it with a new vitality, deepened and softened and humbled and all the rest. But oftentimes, in my experience, this kind of suffering just left a person mangled, limping, breathing more raggedly than before.

Part of my nightly prayer ritual no doubt had something to do with this dynamic. The desire to overcome, to rise from the ashes, to not be decimated by misfortune. And in the end, there was no one and nothing to blame. Blame was the lazy way out. Too easy. Whatever happened in life, the causes were vastly more complex than could ever be fully understood. Things unfolded, very consequential things, and we didn't even know it until it was already done. The grand absurdity of that circumstance. The raw unpredictability of everything. The anarchy of events inside of time. And all of the resulting confusion. What the hell just happened? Who did I think I was? What was the difference between who I thought I was and who I actually was? How had things changed? What must I do now? Where should I go? Who should I be? My entire life could change if I simply did nothing. And so on.

•

In the days after Oscar's diagnoses, I can remember telling myself that I would never be surprised by something terrible happening ever again. The fact that I had been so thunderstruck had felt like a kind of failure. Again I hadn't seen it coming. At my age! After all I'd been through! How many times in my life did I have to get hit with something heartbreaking before I realized that it was baked into the cake? But then this was the very nature of tragedy: the invisibility, the stealth, the power. And how you could never really

217

get ahold of anything except in retrospect, assuming you ever got beyond it at all. And while you were in the midst of it, your best option was probably to accept it, to observe it carefully, to breathe it in and give it your fullest attention, maybe narrate the story as it went along, untangling in real time. Was there any better strategy? Every painful and vexing experience in earthly history had been boiled down into a billion different narratives. A matter of human tradition. Incremental movements toward clarity, one soul at a time. And so now I would take my crack at it. And maybe one day Alice would take hers. Oscar, too. Not that there could ever be anything resembling conventional success in such pursuits. No tidy answers, no finish lines, no trophies. Everything always more complicated than you wished it were. Every little choice you made, tied to a million different outcomes. The overwhelming math of it all. Ungraspable.

·

I continued to kneel in the darkness, eyes closed tight. A man named Brad, middle-aged, alive in an overcrowded desert metropolis at the edge of a country that was rapidly losing its mind. I spent most of my time in my garage, talking to myself, another urban hermit, working to avoid the deadening misery of traffic and the petty inhumanities of office hierarchy, all of the nonsense that we somehow accept as inevitable in the twenty-first century, a matter of mutual enforcement and collective insanity, a flailing defense against emptiness. To be alive in a world that was so often so mean, and so dumb, and so breathtakingly gorgeous, all at the same time, a world that confused profit with value, and fame with success, a world of mountain lions and stock markets and nuclear reactors and rainbows and warring chimpanzees—who wouldn't be a little bit scrambled by such a thing?

Certainly it was doing a number on me. And in response to it I was trying my best to live at odds with the general momentum—not out of bitter hostility, I hoped, but rather in quiet defiance, in pursuit of deepest virtue. I would wake up in my house, and work in my garage, and take care of my family. I would make my silly art and produce my stupid audio documentaries about snack food, and I would lose. I would strip myself down and take myself apart and give myself away, piece by piece. Articulating my confusion. Doing my job. Losing. And before too long I would lose it all. The earth was passing before me. The icecaps were on fire. Here we were. My children would soon be grown. They would head out into the world and would suffer their various wounds, creating their lives on their own terms, making themselves up, just as I was making myself up, one moment at a time. And of course I would want to protect them from every injury, and of course I never could. And this, too, was a form of defeat, possibly the most excruciating loss of all. And on some level I would never get over it, because how could you, and anyway nobody ever got over anything as far as I could tell. Not fully. Not here. But people would make music anyway, and that was the remarkable thing, and probably in the end everything would be fine, just fine, just as the mushroom had tried to explain. And the smallest mountain in the world was called Mt. Wycheproof, a modest granite outcrop in the Terrick Terrick range, all the way down in Victoria, Australia, at the very bottom of the world, exactly where it belonged. We would climb it together someday, I vowed to myself, right then and there, as I knelt on the floor in the darkness of Oscar's room and stared into the glow of my phone. We would stand on that pitiful summit together, all four of us, my family, and someone would take our picture—or maybe we would take it ourselves—and we would post that fucking picture on Instagram, goddamn it all to hell, and everyone would have to love it and know who we were in our glory.

Acknowledgments

I'm indebted to a great many people for their help and support and inspiration through the years. Thank you to my agent, Erin Hosier, and the team at Dunow, Carlson and Lerner for all of your hard work on my behalf. I'm lucky to have you in my corner. Thanks to Robert Lasner, Elizabeth Clementson, and everyone at Ig Publishing, for bringing this novel to life, and for being such generous collaborators. Thank you, Marcy Dermansky, Joseph Grantham, Chelsea Hodson, and Tao Lin, for reading the manuscript and offering insight and encouragement along the way. And thank you, Andrea Bajani and Sam Lipsyte, for your work and kind words. Thank you to the hundreds of writers who have guested on the *Otherppl* podcast over the years. Deepest thanks as well to the show's many listeners, without whom there is no show. Thanks to Steve Almond, Tim O'Brien, Lynne Tillman, Matthew Zapruder, Tenzin Palmo, Thich Nhat Hanh, Hubert Selby Jr., Brad Phillips, Melissa Broder, Mira Gonzalez, Milo Martin, Ben Loory, Duke Haney, Lauren Cerand,

Jarrod Annis, and Dove Shore. Shout-out to my godsons, Oscar Wimmer and Willem VanderMeer. And to my nieces: Madison, Ella, Ali, Sophia, and Isabelle. And my nephew Jake. Thank you to my parents, Frank and Peggy; my sisters, Lauren and Erin; Mark and Jay and Alison and the rest of my extended family and friends. You're too many to name here, but you're in here somewhere. Last but not least, and most of all: Kari, Evan, and River. This book is dedicated to you for good reason. Thank you for everything. I love you so much.